MURDER SO COLD

Eagle Cove Mysteries #2

NORA CHASE

ANNE CHASE

Thomas Publishing

ISBN-13: 978-1-945320-38-5

For first responders everywhere.
Thank you for working so hard to keep us safe.

CHAPTER 1

It's important to state up front, for the record and despite what everyone in Eagle Cove is saying, that I had absolutely no intention of getting caught up in murder and mayhem again.

When it comes to killers and corpses, my extremely firm, crystal-clear, adamantly held viewpoint is: *Been there, survived that, thanks but no thanks.*

I, Sarah Boone, do solemnly swear.

Alas, fate had other plans for me that frigid evening in February. Not that I had any clue as the day unfolded, since most of it unfolded the usual way, with me hustling to keep everything humming along at Emily's Eats, the small cafe I run in downtown Eagle Cove with my dear friend and business partner, Janie McKendrick.

Since opening our doors a month earlier, Janie

and I had been testing different ways of doing things — the "try-and-fail, try-and-succeed" phase of our little business, as we liked to put it. Our current hours of 7:30 a.m. to 5 p.m. seemed to be working, at least for now, with Janie typically arriving early to open the cafe and me staying late to close up. Though our initial offerings were mostly baked goods, come spring we were aiming to expand the menu to include hot breakfasts and a limited lunch selection.

Even with our new business barely off the ground, already we were attracting a loyal clientele thanks to Janie's culinary wizardry. Each day a mix of folks — locals mostly, with a sprinkling of new faces — flowed in for coffees, lattes, scones, and muffins, all of them eager for a cozy escape from the bitter New England cold outside.

Inevitably, however, as the day wound down and the sky faded to dusk, the cafe quieted down. On the frigid February afternoon in question, I found myself alone in the front room, tallying up the day's receipts at the register.

I glanced around the now-empty cafe with a satisfied sigh — another busy day come and gone — then got up from my stool and scooted through the swinging doors into the kitchen, where Janie was boxing up an order. My co-owner is a shy woman, kind and thoughtful by nature, with a lovely face and shoulder-length brown hair she wears in a ponytail. We've been friends for nearly thirty years, ever since she moved to Eagle Cove back in the eighth grade.

I peered at the order slip on the box. "Who's this for?"

"Howard Penn," she replied. "Remember, he came by this morning?"

I thought back and connected the dots. Howard had popped in early and Janie had rung him up at the register while I made two lattes to-go for another customer. "Talkative guy, forties, sandy hair, glasses? Going ice fishing with his buddies?"

"That's the one."

I peeked under the lid and inhaled the lovely aromas of Janie's signature blueberry muffins, maple walnut scones, and chocolate croissants. "Is he a local?"

"I've seen him around a few times, but I think he works in Middlemore." She glanced at her watch and sighed. "I should get these out there if I'm going to get home in time."

"Home in time for what?"

"Ed has the overnight shift tonight, so I'm making an early dinner."

I nodded. Janie's husband Ed was a fireman with irregular hours. "I can deliver the muffins, if you'd like."

Her eyes lit up. "Are you sure?"

"Of course. I'll drive them over after closing up."

"You know where to go?"

"The ice cabins are on the lake near the stretch of shore past the marina, right?"

"Right."

"I should park in the gravel lot near the marina office, then walk out over the ice to the cabin, right?"

"They rented Cabin Three. Their phone number's on the order slip. If you call ahead, they might be able to meet you on the shore."

"How far out on the ice are they?"

"Probably not too far." She looked at me doubtfully. "Sure you don't want me to do this?"

"I'll be fine," I said immediately. "I'll bundle up. I'll wear my boots. The ones that don't slip."

"Okay. Be careful. The wind gets gusty out there."

"I'll be good, I promise." I pointed to my watch. "Time for you to get home."

She gave me a smile. "See you tomorrow morning."

A few minutes later, I flipped the "Open" sign on the front door to "Closed," gave the tables and booths a final wipe-down, and headed back into the kitchen, where my eyes fell on the small desk near the storeroom door. On the desk stood a stack of mail I'd promised myself I'd tackle before the day was done. With my final latte of the day in hand, I sat down, opened my laptop, grabbed the top envelope — oh joy, the gas bill — and dove in.

In the short time since Janie and I had made the life-changing decision to reopen Emily's Eats, I'd learned first-hand that being co-owner of our small business meant being the accountant, waitress, delivery person, plumber, janitor, and so much more. If something broke, I fixed it. If there was a bill to pay, a permit to apply for, an item to source, a mess to clean up, a marketing plan to devise — all of that was on me.

At least I'd had the good sense to partner with the best baker in Eagle Cove. With Janie in charge of the menu and the kitchen — my role was basically to handle everything else — I had every confidence we'd live up to the high standard set by our cafe's original owner and namesake, my dear departed Aunt Emily.

Ah, Emily. I looked up from the laptop screen and sighed. My aunt was indeed dear to me and also departed, though not in the way one typically meant. Once again I found myself wondering how much longer I'd be forced to keep her secret.

Pushing aside that painful and vexatious question, I closed the laptop and stretched my neck. I'd made a nice dent in the stack of mail. But a glance at the box of muffins for our ice-fishing customers reminded me my day's work was not yet done.

A few minutes later, bundled up against the cold, I shut off the lights, locked up for the night, and headed down Main Street to my car, box of muffins in hand. A smile crept to my lips as I realized again how glad I was to be back home in Eagle Cove. As a kid, I'd been eager to escape my hometown and explore the big, wide world. A quarter-century later, as an older and (somewhat) wiser forty-two-year-old, with a daughter in college and a divorce in my rear-view mirror, I had a fuller, richer appreciation of all that life in this small New England town could offer.

Emily's Eats was located on the ground floor of a three-story building in the heart of downtown, along a stretch of blocks filled with shops, restaurants, and other local businesses. Most of the buildings in this part of town dated to the late 1800s and oozed Victorian-era authenticity and charm. Nowadays, that charm was a big draw for tourists who flocked north throughout the year, eager for a taste of Ye Olde New England.

I hopped into my car and pulled out. The road was quiet, with barely any traffic. Though the lake wasn't far from downtown — on a nice day, a pleasant ten-minute walk across the Eagle Cove Common — the drive on this dark winter's night seemed lonely and desolate. The road skirted the

Common and, as the shore drew near, twisted through a thick stand of pine.

Through a clearing in the trees, I glimpsed the shore. A minute later, I pulled into the gravel lot next to the marina office, an old shack used in the summer as a base of operations for boat rentals. Aside from a truck parked at the far end of the lot — my customer Howard's, presumably — the area was deserted. Along the shore I spied two ice cabins resting on the ice, dark and unused.

So where was Cabin Three? I slowly scanned the lake. Though the night sky was clear, the moon and stars weren't offering much light, and it was only with effort that I managed to spot the cabin's silhouette squatting silently on the ice a good five hundred yards away, positioned near a steep and thickly wooded stretch of shoreline.

I took out the order slip from my coat pocket, found Howard's number, and dialed. I was very much hoping that he or one of his buddies would agree to pop out from the ice cabin and retrieve their muffins while I stayed comfy and warm inside my nicely heated car.

The call went immediately to his voicemail. *Grrr.* I tried again and got the same result.

Grrr again. Cell service seemed fine here on shore, but perhaps the service didn't extend onto the lake? If that was the case, then only one person could get Howard his muffins:

Me.

With a final *grrr,* I resigned myself to the inevitable. The walk across the ice would be a long one. Why had I signed up for this?

Because you own a business, that's why. I slipped on my gloves, zipped up my coat, wrapped my scarf around my neck, and turned off the car. "Okay," I said out loud. "You can do this."

I grabbed the box of muffins and clambered out into the cold, dark night, the arctic air biting into my exposed cheeks. Carefully, I made my way across the gravel lot and down the icy, crunchy shoreline to the edge of the lake.

The grey sheet of frozen flatness ahead of me was daunting. I'd done a lot of ice skating as a kid and had once been pretty good at it, but those days were long over. Steeling myself, I took a tentative first step. The ice beneath my boots felt solid and thick, which was good — falling through wouldn't be a concern. But slipping and taking a painful tumble — that was another matter.

Slowly at first but with gradually increasing confidence, I set out. The wind whipped into me, surprising me with its force. Up ahead, the cabin seemed very far away. Even so, with each cautious step, I made steady progress.

As gust after gust barreled by, I realized part of me wasn't upset to be doing this. Part of me, I confess, was curious about what I'd find in the ice fishing cabin. I'd never understood the appeal of this particular activity. As a pastime, it seemed completely, utterly — how to put this kindly …

Pointless.

I shook my head, chastising myself. Was I being unfairly harsh? Was I perhaps not properly appreciating ice fishing's subtle charms? I forced myself to consider the question as I trudged toward my destination. After all, an awful lot of folks seemed to enjoy lugging a floorless shack onto a frozen body of water in the dead of winter for the pleasure of running a fishing line through an ice hole in the hope that some poor fish would bite. Was I missing something?

Nah, I thought with a grin. *Still not hooked.*

As the ice cabin neared, I began to make out details through the gloom. I'd anticipated a decrepit shack, but what I was walking toward was actually a sleek silver trailer, long and narrow, with the floor cut away. Light peeked through a curtained window. The door at the end of the trailer sported a large "3" in black paint.

I reached the aluminum door and knocked. "Muffin delivery!" I called out loudly.

After a moment with no response, I knocked and called out again.

Still no answer.

I frowned. Where were they? I tried recalling what Howard had said earlier. He and his two buddies were spending a couple of nights on the ice — time away from the rat race, he'd proclaimed as he cheerfully placed his order and asked if we could deliver the muffins this evening. "We want 'em as fresh as possible," he'd said.

I sighed. He'd known we'd be delivering. Had he forgotten? I knocked again and leaned closer to listen for movement or music inside.

When I heard nothing, I tried the door. To my surprise, I found it unlocked. Cautiously, I pushed it open and poked my head in. "Hello? It's Sarah from the cafe. I'm here with your muffins."

More silence. I stepped inside. From where I stood, I could see the full length of the cabin.

No one was here.

"Hello?" I said again loudly, hoping I was somehow not seeing them. The entry area was tight, with a small washroom on the left and a storage closet on the right. I made my way inside. A few short steps brought me to the kitchen area, with cabinets and sink to my left and a small table with four chairs to my right.

Past the kitchen, the living area consisted of two sofas facing each other, and past the sofas, anchoring the end of the cabin, were a pair of bunk beds.

And between the sofas, in the center of the floor, was the point of all of this: the ice hole. Three fishing poles rested in stands around the hole with lines in the water. I stepped closer and leaned down for a better look. The ice appeared to be a good foot thick, the lake water at the bottom of the hole dark and still.

I straightened and did a slow swirl, perplexed. The men's duffel bags and coats were strewn about casually. A bag of takeout food from the Golden Dragon, a local restaurant, sat unopened on the kitchen counter. I spied a dark boot print on the ice near the kitchen table.

But the three ice fishermen were nowhere to be seen. Where had they gone? On an errand, perhaps? Had they come to their senses and realized how silly ice fishing was?

The best thing to do, I decided, was to leave the box of muffins and head home. But as I set the box on the dining table, I caught movement out of the corner of my eye.

One of the fishing poles was bending down. Something was hooked!

My pulse quickened. I'd come here to make a delivery, nothing more. This fishing business was none of my concern. I should let the men discover their catch when they returned.

But then I heard myself ask: What if the fish ended up getting caught in the other two lines? Wouldn't the men want me to help them avoid the hassle of getting those lines untangled?

You're just fishing for excuses, my traitorous brain

quickly declared. *Admit it — you're curious. And maybe also wrong about ice fishing having no appeal.*

I'll admit no such thing, I groused to myself. *But I'll cop to being curious. Satisfied?*

Only if you reel in that fish.

I reached down and grabbed the pole. I'd done a tiny amount of fishing as a kid — a very tiny amount — so it took me a few seconds to remember how to do it.

With the pole cradled with one arm, I used my free hand to reel in the line.

The pole bent heavily as the catch drew close. I wasn't sensing a fight — no tugging or pulling from a scared fish fighting for its life. Was the poor thing already exhausted? Had I snagged a log?

In the bottom of the hole, something large appeared. I bent down for a closer look —

And heard myself gasp. A wave of shock — of horror and revulsion — rolled through me.

Staring up at me through the hole —

With open unseeing eyes and a fishing hook through his lip —

Was a man!

My customer, Howard Penn!

Dead!

CHAPTER 2

Those of you who've had the misfortune of being ensnared in a police investigation will know that the next few hours of my life were basically a long, slow, tiring, repetitive slog. As soon as I got to shore and my phone found a signal, I called 911. Then I dashed to my car, started the engine, and cranked the heater, scarcely able to believe what I'd found.

A deluge of random and chaotic thoughts bounced through my head as I waited for the authorities to arrive. Eventually, those thoughts converged on a single undeniable point: Not only was I stunned by what I'd found, I was flummoxed. How had poor Howard ended up beneath the ice? Had the ice somehow cracked open? Where were his two buddies? Had they also fallen through and been lost in the lake?

It was only after trying and failing to solve those stumpers that a new and disturbing thought came: What if what happened wasn't an accident? What if Howard had been *murdered*?

I tensed, surprised I hadn't considered the possibility sooner, especially given all I'd gone through just a few months earlier, when Emily's Eats briefly became a hotspot for homicide.

I was suddenly uncomfortably aware of the fact that I was alone in my car in a deserted parking lot on a cold, dark night. Fear jolted me. I hunkered lower in my seat and locked the door, going on high alert.

Fortunately, Deputy Paul Wilkerson chose that moment to pull up and I sighed with relief. He's a nice young man, fresh out of the academy, just a few years older than my daughter. I got out of my car, hopped into his truck, and told him what I'd found. He had me stay put while he went out to the ice cabin to see for himself. By the time he returned, another young member of the sheriff's department, Deputy Andrea Martinez, had joined us.

I'd just finished telling Deputy Martinez what I'd found — repeating one's story multiple times is an inevitable and annoying part of law enforcement investigations, I'd learned — when a third truck pulled up and Matt jumped out.

As he strode toward me, my heart started thumping.

I suppose I should take a moment to explain. Matt Forysthe is Eagle Cove's sheriff. He was also, once upon a time, my first boyfriend, my first love, my first *everything*.

For me and Matt, "once upon a time" ended twenty-three years ago. That was when, at the tender age of nineteen, deep in my oh-so-wise college sophomore know-it-all phase, I broke up with him. I'd convinced myself I needed to be mature, responsible, and reasonable. Long-distance relationships didn't work, I told myself. If I wanted to grow up, I couldn't hold back. I had to break free of my small-town past and embrace my future.

My only defense is that I was very young.

As is usually the case in the aftermath of such things, Matt and I went our separate ways. We married other people, raised children (two sons for him, a daughter for me), and got divorced.

And now, a quarter-century later, fate found us back in Eagle Cove.

Time had been kind to him. He'd always been handsome, but now he was ruggedly so. His thick, curly brown hair showed just a few flecks of grey. His build, once lean and muscular, was now solid and muscular. He looked every inch the sheriff he'd become.

"Sarah," he said as he reached me. I felt myself flush — I'd always loved how he said my name. His expressive grey eyes drilled into me, his concern palpable.

"I'm fine," I assured him. "A bit shaken, but otherwise fine."

He regarded me for a long moment before nodding, apparently satisfied. "Take me through what happened."

For the third time that night, I described what I'd found. He listened intently, not interrupting. When I finished, he said, "Howard mentioned two buddies, you said?"

"That's right."

"Any sign of them?"

I shook my head. "Their coats and bags were there, I think. But other than that, no."

"Okay." He glanced toward the ice cabin, then turned to Deputy Wilkerson. "Let's get started on Sarah's statement while the details are fresh. We'll have her come in tomorrow to review and sign it."

"Got it."

"I'm going to the cabin. When Doc Barnes arrives, have him join me."

Matt turned to Deputy Martinez. "Let's set up a road block at the entrance to the parking lot."

"Got it," she replied, and headed toward her truck.

Matt squinted as his gaze landed on the truck parked in the darkness at the far end of the lot. He turned to Deputy Wilkerson. "Have you checked that out?"

"Not yet."

"Tell me what you find."

As his deputies moved off to do their jobs, he returned his attention to me. "History repeats, it seems."

I let out a sigh. "I'm getting tired of discovering dead bodies."

There was just enough light from the truck headlights to catch a flash of something — relief? — in his eyes. "Glad to hear that."

In case you're wondering, I wasn't joking and neither was he. When it came to dead bodies, I'd exceeded my quota and then some. Three months earlier, while knocking a hole in a wall in the cafe's basement in search of a leaky pipe, I'd unearthed a mummified corpse. Barely a week later, I'd found Jerry Meachum, a local plumber, murdered in the very same basement. I still had flashbacks to his sightless dead eyes and knew I probably always would.

"The muffins are fresh, by the way," I said, forcing myself to return to the present moment. "I left the box on the table in the cabin. You and your team are welcome to them."

"Thanks." He glanced at my car. "I hate to ask, but…."

"You'd like me to hang out for a while, in case you have questions."

"Sorry."

"Totally understand. Is there anything I can do while I wait? If you'd like, I can call Mario's and order coffee."

"Betsy's already on it," he said, referring to his department's dispatcher. "So I should get out to the…."

"Of course. Go. I'm good."

With apparent reluctance, he turned and made his way across the lot to Deputy Wilkerson, who was running a flashlight over the truck. After conferring with him for a moment, Matt headed out onto the ice.

And then it was slog time. Deputy Wilkerson had me repeat my story again while he slowly scribbled notes for my statement. Doc Barnes, the town's coroner, arrived and joined Matt in the ice cabin. The boat rental shack's owner pulled in and opened the shack for use as a temporary field office. A crime scene technician arrived with the ambulance. Finally, Matt returned from the cabin, updated his team (out of my earshot, unfortunately), then told me I could go home.

As I was heading out, another car pulled up at the roadblock. Behind the wheel was Wendy Danvers, a reporter for the *Eagle Cove Gazette*. Her eyes locked on mine.

Great, I thought. *Just what I needed now — more questions.*

My phone buzzed twice on the short drive home. As soon as I pulled into a parking spot in front of the cafe, I checked to see who the calls were from — Wendy, both of them — and shut off the phone.

I was relieved and a bit surprised that Mom hadn't called yet. For the moment, at least, Eagle Cove's gossip network was behind the curve, a fact for which I was grateful. The last thing I needed right now was to rehash what I'd just spent the last two hours rehashing.

As I made my way into the cafe building and trudged up the stairs to my apartment on the third floor, a wave of exhaustion rolled through me. I wasn't even sure how I honestly, truly felt about all of this, I realized. My brain was a jumble, my stomach knotted with tension.

I slid my key into the apartment lock. As the door opened before me, I found myself trembling. From the moment of discovery, I'd been keeping a lid on my emotions so I could stay focused and clear-headed for Matt and his team. But no matter how hard I tried to remain stoic in the face of unexplained death, the reality of it couldn't be ignored. In the end, there was no getting around a simple, basic truth:

Finding corpses was no fun.

I breathed in and out, waiting for the rush of emotion to subside. Quietly, I shut the door behind me and set my keys on the entry foyer table. What I was experiencing wasn't grief, at least not exactly. Howard Penn wasn't a friend. I'd known him only as a customer. Still, he was a fellow human being, and now he was dead. Though I'd barely known him, it was natural to feel bad for him.

It was then that I finally identified the emotion lurking in the background, surging quietly beneath the distress and the sadness:

Relief.

The last time I'd discovered dead bodies, I'd had a personal connection.

This time around, aside from the bad luck of delivering muffins at the wrong time, *I wasn't involved.*

As if a stopper had been pulled loose, I felt tension flowing from me. This time around, I didn't need to solve any puzzles. I didn't need to devise plans and make things happen.

Instead of diving into this evening's shocking event, I could focus on other things, like the unavoidable fact that right now, at this very moment, my mind and body were crying out for *sleep*.

Yes, *sleep*. The bed beckoned. The simple act of acknowledging my non-connection to Howard's death made me feel lighter.

Comforted by that reassuring thought, I padded into the bedroom, slipped into my nightgown, climbed under the covers, and almost immediately fell into blessedly dreamless (and corpseless) slumber.

CHAPTER 3

I awoke before dawn to the sound of pounding at my front door.

Heart thumping, I bolted upright, shot a glance at my bedside clock —

And groaned.

It was 7:07 a.m. Which meant I was *late*. Usually I tried to be in the cafe by seven.

As the events of the previous night came flooding back, I heard more knocks, with an urgency I felt in my bones.

Not bothering with my bathrobe or slippers, I hurried in my nightgown to the front door, looked through the keyhole —

And groaned again.

"Mom," I said loudly through the closed door.

"Open this door *right now*, Sarah," my mother said firmly.

After my third groan of the morning — I needed to put a cap on the groaning, I decided then and there — I accepted the inevitable and yanked open the door.

Mom stared at me with dismay. "Oh, Sarah."

"I know. I'm running late. I'm sorry."

To my surprise, she pulled me in for a long and overly tight hug. "It's the shock, isn't it? Oh, how horrible it must have been."

I realized she was talking about Howard and the ice cabin.

"Why didn't you answer when I phoned?" she asked, squeezing tighter. "I was so worried."

"I'm fine, Mom," I said, extricating myself carefully. "Really, I'm good."

"You just woke up, didn't you?"

"I was exhausted."

Her concerned eyes took in every inch of me. "And now, with everyone downstairs waiting…."

I blinked. "Waiting?"

"For you, of course."

And that's when it hit me — and I let out my biggest groan yet.

Somehow I had forgotten that today was the day of …

The dreaded photo shoot.

Mom's gaze was sympathetic. "Power shower. I'll get your clothes ready."

With a gentle push, she aimed me at the

bathroom, where I raced through my regular morning routine in record time. The instant I emerged, Mom took me by the hand and sat me at the dining table. "I'll do your makeup."

"Mom —"

"The light is good here. Plus, I'm faster and you know it."

I sighed and gave in. In quick order, Mom slapped foundation, mascara and lipstick on me, her movements deft and efficient.

"You're sure about the makeup?" I said, though I knew it was futile.

"Very sure. You want to look your best. Speaking of...." She paused to touch up a spot on my left cheek. "You know I like your hair. But you know what would look lovely on you? A nice bob. Sally does a terrific job with bobs."

I stared at Mom (and her stylish auburn bob) with my usual mixture of love and exasperation. As moms go, she's the best — warm and expressive and caring and full of energy. With her sparkling green eyes and lovely laugh, she lights up any room she's in.

But she's also — how to put this gently — prone to maternal prodding and protectiveness. When she decides what's best or safest for me, she pushes.

And my usual instinct is to push back.

I squelched the urge to remind her that I was actually quite fond of my shoulder-length brown hair. It had taken me years to figure out how to style and color it, and I had no intention of abandoning the fruits of my labors now.

But now was not the time to get into that.

"How late am I?" I asked.

"Don't worry. I texted Janie. We'll be down there in no time."

"I can't believe I forgot."

"You've just been through an ordeal. How late did Matthew keep you?"

"A couple of hours."

Mom frowned. "Betsy told me he was there all night."

I nodded, unsurprised. Betsy, the police dispatcher, was one of Mom's closest friends and a key player in the Eagle Cove gossip network. "What else did she tell you?"

"She said Matthew doesn't know what to make of it. He isn't pleased."

And with that, Mom stood me up, urged me into my work clothes — comfortable sneakers, jeans, and white blouse — and ushered me out of the apartment and down the stairs.

In the ground-floor hallway, I paused, steeling myself for what was coming next, then stepped into the cafe.

"Good morning, everyone," I said with as much cheer as I could muster. "Sorry I'm late."

My eyes landed on Gerry Byrne, the

photographer, setting up his camera equipment in the center of the cafe. A ginger-haired Irishman in his forties, he was a mid-morning regular — large black coffee and cinnamon roll — which he invariably took with him to his photography studio a few doors down on Main Street.

He glanced up from fiddling with his lighting umbrella. "Morning, Sarah," he said with his pleasing Irish lilt. "You're just in time. Be ready for you and Janie in a bit."

"Thanks, Gerry."

Standing next to him was the front room's other occupant — Eagle Cove's formidable mayor, Doris Johnson.

"Sarah," the mayor said as she stepped toward me, her expression sympathetic. "I'm sorry to hear what you went through last night."

"Thank you," I replied. The mayor was a tall woman in her late fifties, with short black hair tinged with grey and smooth ebony skin that didn't show her age. She came across as no-nonsense and determined, which is exactly what she was. Mom worked as her office manager and loved the job because, as she put it, "The mayor thinks ahead and knows what she wants and keeps everyone on their toes, including me, and that's a good thing."

The mayor's eyes held mine. "If you're not feeling up to the shoot this morning…."

"I'm fine," I said immediately. "Sorry I was late getting down here."

"No worries," she replied. "I'm just glad you're here."

Like much of what happened in Eagle Cove, the photo shoot was the mayor's brainchild. A relentless business booster, she'd decided the cafe should be included in a promotional campaign she'd dreamed up to lure tourists to our small New England town.

Mom ran an eye over me. "You'll need your apron, the one with 'Emily's Eats' on the front."

"It's in the kitchen, freshly washed and pressed. Back in a sec." I scooted behind the counter and into the kitchen, where I found Janie pulling a tray of blueberry scones from the oven.

"Morning," Janie said as she set the tray in the pastry rack to cool. "Gerry said he'll be ready for us in a few minutes."

"Sorry I'm late. Hopefully we can finish up with the photos before the morning rush starts."

Janie turned to give me her full attention. Like me, she was wearing makeup this morning. I examined her face for spots needing touchup.

"I'm the one who's sorry," she said.

"For what?"

"For letting you go to the lake last night."

"Oh, nonsense," I said, batting away her concern. "I volunteered, remember?"

Janie's anxiety was undiminished. "You sure you're okay?"

"I'm fine," I insisted.

"Even after everything that happened last fall?"

I took hold of her hands and gave them a squeeze. "I'm fine. Promise."

She gave me a short, searching glance. "Then I guess we should...."

"The sooner we get this over with, the better."

"How do I look?"

"You look great," I said approvingly. "A bit of touchup on the right side of your lips and you're ready."

She took a compact from her apron pocket to examine her face. "Thank you."

After slipping into my "Emily's Eats" apron, I made my way with Janie to the front of the cafe, where we surrendered ourselves to Gerry's attentions.

"Let's try near the front window," he said.

Behind him, Mayor Johnson and Mom nodded their agreement. After a few shots, Gerry shook his head and moved us to one of the red vinyl booths along the wall. After another frown, he arranged us behind the cash register.

"I'm not feeling it yet," he said. "Let's try in front of the display case."

Dutifully, Janie and I positioned ourselves in

front of the display case, which was full of Janie's delicious muffins, croissants, pies, and cookies.

"That's what we want," he said. "The two of you look terrific."

"Remember to smile, Sarah," Mom said.

I placed a smile on my face.

"Good," Gerry said, snapping away.

The bell on the cafe's front door signaled the morning's first customer. I resisted the urge to frown when I saw it was Wendy, our ace reporter.

Wendy wasn't a regular — she avoided carbs like the plague, she'd informed me more than once — so seeing her at this early hour meant just one thing: I was about to get grilled.

"Morning, everyone," she said to the room. "Okay if I observe? The paper's doing a story on the promotional campaign."

"That's wonderful," Mayor Johnson said, eyeing her carefully. "A news story about the promotional campaign will be very helpful in getting the word out."

Wendy reached into her purse and pulled out her notebook and a tape recorder. An attractive woman a few years younger and ten pounds slimmer than me, she had shoulder-length brown hair and a doggedness that served her well in her job. "Thank you. Mayor Johnson, can you share a bit about what you're planning?"

The mayor cleared her throat. "The campaign

will run in four phases — one per quarter — and highlight the seasonal activities that make Eagle Cove a wonderful place to visit throughout the year."

Wendy scribbled down notes. "What are you promoting for winter visitors?"

"Proximity to the ski resorts, of course. After a day on the slopes, downtown Eagle Cove offers a tempting array of restaurants and shops. The trails on Heartsprings Ridge just outside of town are excellent for cross-country skiing and hiking. We're also fortunate to have nearby orchards and sugarhouses open for tours year-round. And of course, Heartsprings Lake is perfect for ice skating and … other activities."

The mayor had almost said "ice fishing" but had stopped herself.

Wendy's gaze flickered toward me. "Sarah, how do you feel about Emily's Eats being included in the promotional campaign?"

I knew what was hiding behind that question but kept my tone upbeat. "As a new business in downtown Eagle Cove, we're thrilled and honored to be included."

"Any concerns about the recent violence that took place here and how that might impact your business?"

The room tensed. The ambush had begun. No one needed to ask what Wendy was referring to.

I cleared my throat. "Our focus now is on doing everything we can to make Emily's Eats a big success."

"And when you say *everything*," Wendy said, stretching out the word, "does that include honing your skill at discovering dead bodies?"

"Wendy," I said, taken aback.

"Sarah," she replied. "I know you were at the lake last night when the three dead men were discovered."

"Three?" I gasped.

She smiled, pleased to be relaying new information, and consulted her notes. "Howard Penn, Alan Petersen, and Daniel Potter. I take it you're the one who called it in?"

"I —"

"And I take it you saw only one body?"

"I —"

"And I take it you went out there to deliver an order of … muffins?"

I felt it then — the stirrings of anger. "If you already know all of this, then there's no need to ask."

"These men were your customers, correct?"

"I'm pretty sure that's not relevant."

Wendy's eyes glittered. "Are you saying you're not concerned about your cafe's connections to multiple deaths?"

"Wendy —"

"Three months ago, a murder took place in this very building. You were instrumental in catching the killer. A week before that, you unearthed a corpse, also here. And now three of your customers are dead, under very suspicious circumstances."

Mayor Johnson stepped in, her displeasure clear. "Ms. Danvers, the past is the past. The unfortunate events of last fall have been the subject of extensive and thorough reporting by the *Gazette*. I fail to see the point of rehashing all that yet again."

Wendy frowned. "There's a lot more to that story."

The mayor's eyebrows rose. "Ms. Danvers —"

Wendy shook her head. "No, Mayor Johnson, I will not be dissuaded. What happened last fall is just the tip of the iceberg. The deaths of the three men on the lake are linked. The complete story has yet to be told."

She swiveled back to me, her expression full of challenge and defiance.

"The truth needs to come out. And I intend to be the one to tell it."

CHAPTER 4

Here's the thing about "the truth." I'm a big fan — a huge fan. I love knowing what's what. On occasion, I can be a tad inquisitive myself.

So as Wendy stared me down, practically daring me to reveal what I knew, part of me sympathized with her frustration.

Because Wendy Danvers, ace reporter for the *Eagle Cove Gazette*, was right about there being a whole lot more to the story.

The part she knew went as follows: Ten years back, a woman named Amy killed a man named Peter and fooled my dear Aunt Emily, who owned the cafe, into believing that the killing was in self-defense. Amy then persuaded my aunt to hide Peter's body behind a wall in the building's basement.

Fast-forward to three months ago, shortly after

Aunt Emily's funeral. As the building's new owner, I knocked a hole in the basement wall in search of a leaky pipe and discovered Peter's corpse. Upon hearing the news, Amy returned to town, disguised as a real-life psychic named Hialeah. After a local plumber named Jerry recognized her beneath her disguise, Amy lured Jerry to the basement and killed him. Then she very nearly killed me and two others. It was only through the sheerest chance that I turned the tables on Amy and survived.

After her capture, word circulated that Amy and Peter were con artists who'd had a falling out. Very quickly, the Eagle Cove gossip network absorbed and accepted the idea that Amy had returned to Eagle Cove in search of money that Peter had hidden.

The story was a good one in the sense that it provided reasonable answers for most of what had gone down. I'd played a major part in ensuring the story circulated and took hold.

But the truth of the matter was that the con-artist story was a complete and total crock.

In reality, the con-artist story was cover for a much deeper deception.

A deception involving people I loved, including Aunt Emily and my childhood best friend, Claire.

A deception I had zero interest in sharing with a certain *Gazette* reporter.

"Wendy," I said. "We've been over this."

"Oh, I know," Wendy said. "And I get that you're not ready to share. But you will be. And when you are, I'll be here."

"Sure," I said, trying to sound disappointed yet at the same time patient and forgiving, like the way one acts when someone you're fond of repeats something kooky for the millionth time.

At that point, Gerry stepped in and got me and Janie refocused on the shoot. Wendy watched for a few moments and left. A few poses later, Gerry declared he had the shots he needed. Mayor Johnson thanked everyone and headed out, Mom in tow. Gerry packed up his equipment and did the same.

And just like that, Emily's Eats returned to normal. The usual rhythms reasserted themselves. Customers flowed in for their morning croissants and lattes, and Janie and I rushed to keep up.

Except, I gradually realized, the sense of normalcy was an illusion.

The first indicator of ongoing disruption was the early arrival of my neighbor and second-floor tenant, Gabby McBride, a sharp-tongued octogenarian with a fondness for bright floral print dresses and a cane she used mainly as a weapon. Most mornings, Gabby shuffled in a few minutes before nine and commandeered the red booth nearest the front door, from which she and "the girls," as she referred to them — a trio of fellow octogenarians known individually as Mrs. Bunch, Mrs. Chan, and Ms. Hollingsworth — held court.

But Gabby was a good half-hour early and it didn't take a genius to suss out why.

"Sarah," she said solicitously, a tone she used only when she wanted something. Her gaze radiated sympathy and kindness, confirming my suspicions. "You poor, poor thing."

I tried not to smile. "I'm fine, Gabby."

"Of course you are. A pillar of strength. Tower of power. Solid as a rock. Always have been, that's what I tell everyone."

"Can I get you your usual?"

"You are so brave." Before I could turn, she gripped my arm. "After you get me my mocha, you're gonna sit down and unburden yourself. It isn't healthy to hold back. I'm here for you. Lay your troubles on me — I can take 'em. That's what friends are for."

I smiled. "Thank you."

As I got her latte ready, I heard the hallway door open and glanced over to see the building's other tenant, Mr. Benson, step inside.

I let out a small sigh. Mr. Benson was early as well. A careful, fastidious man in his early seventies, he invariably popped in at nine on the dot and perused three different newspapers — print editions, of course — while slowly consuming a pot of Earl Grey tea and a cranberry scone.

"Good morning, Sarah," he said as he settled into his customary seat at the counter, in easy earshot of Gabby in case she wanted to pester him about something, which she often did.

"Tea and scone coming right up," I said.

As I busied myself with their orders, I sensed their impatience, which they were barely holding in check.

I was finishing Gabby's latte when the cafe's front door swept open and my next morning disruption arrived in the form of Hialeah Truegood, a professional medium who had recently moved to Eagle Cove from New Orleans.

Hialeah was, truth be told, a puzzle I hadn't even begun to decipher. I'd first met her — or rather, a version of her — the previous fall, when Amy the killer returned to Eagle Cove disguised as Hialeah. Shortly after Amy was hauled off to jail, the real-life Hialeah astonished all of us by walking into the cafe and announcing that the spirits had sent her north because her help would be needed in Eagle Cove.

A slim woman in her early forties with a lustrous tumble of shoulder-length red hair, she favored silk gowns that fit snugly around her waist and flowed to the floor. Her makeup was on the heavy side but always expertly applied. Despite her dramatic appearance, her manner was invariably soft and polite, her voice low and musical, with a Southern accent I found very appealing.

For several hours each day, from her preferred table near the front window, Hialeah performed psychic readings for a steady stream of paying clients. In hushed tones that were difficult to overhear, she consulted tarot cards and offered insights gleaned from, as she put it, "our departed loved ones."

I honestly didn't know what to make of her. When it came to mediums, my standard assumption was that most were unscrupulous frauds — adept at observation, skilled at conveying empathy, and sadly willing to exploit human grief and anxiety for personal gain.

But Hialeah didn't fit that judgmental box. For one thing, I liked her, and my instincts about people were usually pretty good. For another, she had an uncanny knack for saying things that later turned out to be kinda-sorta true.

"Sarah," she said breathlessly as she shut the cafe door behind her. Normally she was calm and unruffled, but this morning she seemed almost agitated.

"Is something wrong, Hialeah?"

"Yes, I've —" she said, then stopped when she realized Gabby and Mr. Benson were hanging on her every word. "I see you're busy right now.

Perhaps we can talk later, when you have a free moment?"

"Sure, no problem."

I brought Gabby her latte and was debating whether to accede to her demand for a full rundown of the previous night's ice-cabin business when my phone buzzed.

I pulled it from my pocket and saw with a jolt that it was Matt.

"Hey," I said when I picked up. "Heard you had a late one."

"That I did." His voice was scratchy, probably from being out in the cold all night.

"What's up?"

I heard a quiet sigh, which I knew from experience meant he'd reached a decision he wasn't fully comfortable with. "Can you come out to the ice cabin?"

"Sure. When?"

"Now."

"Right now?" I said, surprised.

"Yes." There was an undercurrent of urgency in his tone. "You and I need to talk."

CHAPTER 5

A few minutes later, after conferring with Janie and calling Mom to ask her to fill in at the register, I slipped two of Matt's favorites — a blueberry scone and a chocolate chip muffin — into a bag, hopped into my car, and headed to the lake.

In the pale light of day, the Victorian-era buildings along Main Street seemed effortlessly quaint and comforting. The Eagle Cove Common, lightly dusted with snow, exuded serenity. As I wound my way through the stand of pine trees near the lake, the soft sunlight filtering through the branches struck me as beautiful, even ethereal.

All of which served to reinforce how unreal it was to be on my way to the scene of three suspicious deaths. Unpleasantness wasn't supposed to happen in places like Eagle Cove. Cafe owners like me weren't supposed to discover dead bodies while delivering muffins.

The disconnects didn't end there. Eagle Cove's recent bounty crop of corpses barely held a candle to a truth about this town that I'd only recently become aware of — a truth so bizarre, perplexing, and incongruous that it continued to stun and baffle me, months after it was unearthed in shocking fashion.

For reasons I couldn't begin to fathom, my quiet New England hometown was secretly a hotbed of —

Espionage.

The very idea was ludicrous, of course — cue the movie soundtrack. Silly, ridiculous, eyebrow-raising, snort-inducing — yes, yes, yes, *yes*.

Because — *come on.* Spies hung out in glamorous places like Paris or technological places like Silicon Valley or political places like Washington.

Not in cute little New England tourist towns like Eagle Cove.

Yet I'd come face to face with the indisputable proof.

My dear Aunt Emily, who for decades had been a cafe owner and Eagle Cove mainstay, was in fact a retired spy.

My childhood best friend Claire had joined the same secret spy agency after college.

And Amy, the killer I'd tangled with? She and

Peter had been spies as well, on the run from nameless adversaries and hiding out in Eagle Cove, when Amy betrayed Peter and her agency and sold top-secret information to an unnamed enemy. A decade later, Amy had returned to Eagle Cove to search for more of that secret information, which Peter had apparently hidden before he was killed.

All of this had come to light the previous fall, soon after I returned to Eagle Cove for the funeral of Aunt Emily, who I believed had died in a tragic car crash. In the space of two short weeks, while grieving the loss of my aunt, I'd been forced to deal with a ruthless killer, two dead bodies, decades-old secrets, and — yes — *spies.*

I'd barely begun absorbing all these revelations when the most stunning twist of all was revealed.

Shortly after Amy's capture, my childhood friend (and now government agent) Claire had handed me a blindfold and driven me to a secret facility located somewhere outside Eagle Cove. Once there, she'd guided me into an elevator, down a hallway, and into a hospital room with a bed and beeping machines.

Three months had passed since that fateful day, but even now, I found myself shaking my head in disbelief as I recalled the moment I came face to face with the impossible:

Aunt Emily, still alive.

"Have a seat, Sarah," my aunt told me that day. "We have much to discuss."

Blinking back tears, I did as instructed, slowly lowering myself into the chair next to her bed as I gazed upon the woman I had believed was dead.

Bandages covered the left side of her thin, angular face. Her visible cheek showed signs of bruising. Her left arm was wrapped in a sling.

But the look she was giving me — oh, my heart sang.

Aunt Emily was *here*. Still with us. Still alive. Still full of fight.

"You're dead," I whispered. "You were killed."

"I very nearly was," she replied.

I reached out and gently took hold of her hand. Her skin was cool to the touch. She squeezed back.

"How did you survive?" I whispered.

"Luck. Plain and simple."

"Tell me what happened. Matt told me he found evidence your car was hit by another car."

Emily nodded. "I was chased and forced off the road."

I gasped. "By Amy?"

"Yes."

"And then…."

"My car tumbled off the ridge road and I lost consciousness."

"Then how…?"

Behind me, Claire spoke up. "My colleagues

went to investigate and, when they found her alive, rescued her and brought her here."

"You've been here for the past two weeks?"

Emily spoke up. "I regained consciousness two days ago."

"Two days ago?" I repeated. "That means you were…."

"In a medically induced coma, I'm told, to give me a better chance to heal."

I focused on her face and then her arm. "How badly are you hurt?"

"Badly," she said matter-of-factly. "My arm is broken in three places. My shoulder and ribs are cracked. I suffered a concussion. My forehead will require surgery to fix what might otherwise be a rather noticeable scar. In short, my recovery will take time and effort."

I turned to Claire. "So to cover up what happened to Emily, your colleagues put a dead body in Emily's car and torched it?"

"Yes," Claire said.

I had a million questions — a billion questions — about how her agency managed to do all that, but my most urgent focus was on the woman who had somehow, despite the odds, survived.

She regarded me quietly, her grey eyes as alert as ever. "I understand you know about my past."

"You mean, about you being a spy? Yes."

"You know about Claire as well, of course."

"Along with Amy and Peter."

"Tell me what you think, now that you know."

"I think," I started, then stopped as I realized the emotions and questions rushing through me were anything but clear.

"I think a lot of things," I began.

"Tell me about each one," Emily replied. "One at a time."

"I'm grateful and amazed you're alive. I still can't believe I'm talking with you. I went to your funeral. I *organized* your funeral."

"Thank you for that," she said, a twinkle in her eyes. "I'm sure it was very well done."

"The turnout was terrific. The place was packed. The mayor gave a wonderful speech."

"I must admit I'm glad I wasn't there. What else are you feeling?"

"Surprise and shock, of course."

"Of course."

"Also relief in knowing what the deal really is. Things that bugged me — no, more than that, things that really bothered and upset me — are finally starting to make sense."

"Things such as?"

"Well, things such as Claire." I glanced back at the sleek, sophisticated, stylish woman who had once been my best friend. "For twenty years now, ever since college, I've been angry at Claire for shutting me out of her life. I didn't understand why she did that. Now I do."

"Our line of work is never without sacrifice," Emily said. "Tell me what else you are feeling."

"I guess I feel kind of … stupid."

"Why?"

"Because I didn't know. I mean, until a few days ago, I had no idea. Even though the clues were there. If I'd been paying more attention…."

"Sarah," Emily said firmly. "That line of thinking isn't helpful to you or anyone."

"I know, but…."

"Clues aren't clues until you know there's a mystery."

"Maybe," I said with a sigh. She was right, of course, but I wasn't ready to accept that, at least not yet.

"What else, Sarah?" she asked calmly.

"Guilt," I said.

"Because?"

"Because I couldn't save Jerry Meachum."

Emily gave my hand a squeeze. "Jerry was a kind, helpful, good-hearted man. I'm very sorry he got caught up in this."

I pushed back an upwelling of emotion. "His memorial service was yesterday. And unlike your service, I know his was the real deal. Because I found him dead on the basement floor."

"I'm so sorry that happened. I feel bad about my role in this."

"Your role?" I said, unsure what she meant. "You were in a medically induced coma."

Emily shook her head. "Everything that happened in Eagle Cove over the past few weeks is the result of a mistake I made many years ago."

"By mistake, you mean how Amy fooled you."

Emily blinked back tears and my eyes welled up in sympathy.

"Yes, Sarah. Bluntly and well put. A decade ago, Amy fooled me. She spun a tale and I was taken in. Her story preyed upon certain ... misgivings I've harbored about the organization that once employed me. I'm choosing to speak in generalities because it's better for you — safer for you — to not know specifics."

"I get that. But what happened in Eagle Cove wasn't your fault. It was Amy's."

"I agree, largely. It's important for you to agree with that as well. The guilt you feel about Jerry is misplaced."

I shrugged. "On a rational level, I don't disagree. Amy's the one who killed Jerry and almost killed you and me and Claire."

"Yes."

"Amy's responsible for all of that. Not you, not me."

"Yes."

"But here's the thing. Unlike you, I was on the scene. I could have — should have — figured it out sooner."

My aunt shook her head. "No, you couldn't have. You were on the scene, yes. But you lacked the information required."

"A clue isn't a clue until you know there's a mystery?"

"Exactly."

Behind me, Claire stirred. "We'll have to wrap things up in the next few minutes, I'm afraid. Emily needs her rest."

"Of course," I said. "I'll come back tomorrow."

"About that," Claire said. "That won't be possible."

I turned toward her, surprised. "Why?"

"Now that Emily's awake and stable, she's being transferred to a different hospital to accelerate her recovery."

"Which hospital?"

Claire looked at me guiltily. "I can't tell you."

"Nearby?"

She shook her head. "In a different state."

"Sarah," Emily said firmly, trying to nip my objection in the bud. "Please do not get upset with Claire. She pulled innumerable strings to obtain approval for this visit."

"But...."

"The facility will provide excellent care and aid me in my recovery."

I was glad Emily would be well cared for, and I accepted what Claire had done to make this visit possible. But inside, a well of emotion was rushing upward. What they were telling me — it felt wrong somehow. It felt —

"It's not fair," I blurted out, unable to stop myself.

Emily's eyes misted up. "Sarah...."

"I just got you back and now you're going away again?"

"I'm sorry, but yes."

I swallowed my anger. After a moment, I managed to say, in a calmer tone, "I get that your recovery is the priority. If you'll get the best care in this other place, then I'm all for it."

"I'm glad to hear that."

"But I want to spend more time with you before you go."

Emily glanced at Claire. "I understand. We have several more items to discuss."

"What items?"

"The first," Emily said, "is a request from the organization."

"Still no name for this mysterious organization, I see." After pausing to allow Emily or Claire to volunteer a name, I sighed. "I guess I should accept that I may never know which super-secret spy agency is involved in all of this. Claire and I have been agreeing to pretend that I believe it's the CIA."

Emily's eyes flashed with appreciation. "I understand you kept information about the existence of the organization to yourself when you were questioned by the sheriff and his deputies."

"That's right."

"Why did you not share that information?"

"Because I didn't need to."

Her gaze sharpened. "Explain."

"I knew Amy and Claire weren't going to tell anyone about the spy angle. And I realized that the story you told Gabby and Mr. Benson a decade ago — the story about Peter being a wife beater who attacked you, requiring you to defend yourself — could continue to hold up, with enhancements."

"Tell me about the enhancements."

"The new story is, Amy and Peter were con artists with warrants for fraud and identity theft in multiple states. Ten years ago, they stole something, probably money, and hid out in Eagle Cove. They had a falling out and Amy killed Peter. Then Amy conned you into believing her tale of domestic abuse and convinced you to help her hide Peter's body."

"So in this new story, I was duped."

"Yes," I said. "Sorry."

Emily sighed. "The truth is, duped I was. Not

exactly as described in your enhanced story — a good one, by the way — but in the essential aspect."

"Meaning … you believed Amy when she told you she was in danger and a potential victim?"

"Yes."

"From what you said earlier, I sense you're not a fan of the organization you once worked for…."

"That is correct."

"But now they're helping you to recover…."

"Yes, they are."

"In exchange for what?"

Emily's eyes flashed again. "I'm afraid I can't tell you that."

"So…." I let the silence linger, hoping she or Claire would say more. But they were masters at this game and all of us knew it, so I gave up. "Tell me about the request."

"The organization would like to rent the studio apartment in your building in downtown Eagle Cove."

"They want to *what*?" I said, surprised.

"A two-year lease with an option to renew, paid in full up front, fifty percent above market rate."

When Claire told me the number, I gasped. The cafe — which I'd just decided to reopen with Janie — had a fix-it list a mile long. The money would come in very handy.

"Who would my tenant be?"

Claire said, "Mostly, people who aren't part of

the organization. Experts in a variety of fields. Some know about the organization, but most of them don't."

"I suppose I shouldn't ask why your organization needs a studio apartment in a small tourist town in northern New England."

"The less you know…."

"The better. Okay, fine. I get it. Top-secret national security blah blah blah."

Claire smiled. "Does that mean the answer is yes?"

"Well," I said, "it's really not for me to say."

"Meaning?"

"I don't own the building. I didn't inherit it. The person who willed it to me isn't dead."

Claire inhaled slowly and turned to Emily.

"Sarah," Emily said. "About that."

I tensed and swiveled back to my aunt. "Aunt Emily, what's going on?"

Her gaze was steady. "I said we have several items to discuss."

"Yes, you said that."

"The next item is this. We need you to keep today's conversation to yourself."

"Meaning what?"

"No one can know I'm alive."

I found myself shaking my head. "No."

Emily's eyes widened. "Why not?"

"Because you're here! You're alive!"

"Sarah...."

"We'll come up with a story. It'll be a crazy story, but we'll figure it out and make it work."

"I'm afraid that's not possible."

"Why?"

"Because I'm needed, apparently," Emily said, her voice trembling. "My services are once again required."

"For some new top-secret mission? Which you can't tell me about?"

"Yes."

"You quit the organization decades ago. They have no right to drag you back."

"That is correct," Emily said, her voice rising. "They have no such right. But certain events have transpired that require the involvement of someone with my knowledge and skills."

I grunted with frustration. It was all so maddeningly vague. And even though I understood why it had to be, I still hated it.

"Someone else can do it."

"Sadly, no." Emily said.

I wasn't ready to give up. "Eagle Cove needs you, too. Your family needs you."

"The town and you will do fine without me."

"But what about Mom?"

Emily suddenly looked stricken. "How is Nancy?"

I took a deep breath, very aware that what I

said next could hurt and worry Emily. "Mom took your death very hard. She's holding up well, but she misses you. A lot."

Tears filled Emily's eyes. "I miss her terribly."

"Isn't there a way for her to come see you?"

Emily slowly shook her head. "I'm afraid not. She's … how to put this."

"A sharer?"

Emily nodded sadly. "Yes."

"You're worried she'll blab."

"I'm afraid so, yes. Not deliberately, of course. But…."

I didn't know how to respond because, frankly, I understood Emily's concern. Mom was expressive — it was part of her nature. She didn't really know how to hold back.

"Well, you need to find a way." I turned to Claire. "You're both smart, capable women. So here's the deal. I'll keep your secret for now. But not permanently."

Claire's mouth tightened. "What happened here has to remain here."

"It will. Temporarily. Until you figure out a new and better plan. A plan that allows Mom and Emily to see each other again. A plan you're going to come up with and put in place very soon."

I rose to my feet. The two of them stared at me, neither uttering a word. The silence seemed to go on and on.

But this time, I waited for them to talk.

Finally, Claire said, "Okay. We'll work out something."

"Good," I said, keeping my tone level despite feeling a rush of triumph. "You said there are several items to discuss. What's the next one?"

"From time to time," Claire said, "we may ask for your help."

"What kind of help?"

"Small things. Someone may ask you to place a call. Someone may ask you to store an item for them. That kind of thing."

"Sure," I said immediately, still buzzing from successfully negotiating for Mom to see Emily again. "There's a spy word for that, right?"

Claire frowned. "A spy word?"

"Dead drop? Is that it? Am I a dead drop?"

"No," Claire said, her mouth twitching to hide a smile. As annoyed as she was with me for forcing her to agree to find a way for Mom to see Emily, she was also amused by my curiosity.

"Most certainly not a dead drop," Emily added, in a warning tone that both of us knew extremely well. "Claire neglected to add that it's highly unlikely you'll ever be asked to do anything."

"Right," Claire said. "Highly unlikely."

I turned to Emily. "I don't want you to worry about me. I'm going to be fine."

My aunt's eyes drilled into me. "I have every

confidence in you, Sarah. I cannot say the same about the organization I resigned from thirty years ago. Circumstances may necessitate your rare involvement, but my very firm preference is for you to remain outside this organization's purview."

There was a finality in her tone, like a big decision had just been made.

I became aware of the time. My aunt was tired and hurt and in pain and needed rest. I'd always thought of her as a superwoman, but she wasn't. She was an eighty-three-year-old with broken bones who had barely survived a car crash and had just emerged from two weeks in a medically induced coma.

"I should get going," I said. "You need your rest."

Emily shook her head. "Not before you answer three more questions."

Claire said, "You have a…."

Emily cut her off. "He'll have to wait." She beckoned for me to sit back down, then reached out and took my hand. "Tell me how Anna is doing in college."

I smiled. "Her freshman year is going well. She and her roommate get along great. She aced her mid-terms and joined a school environmental group."

"How does she feel about your decision to move to Eagle Cove?"

"She's happy for me, I think. She'll spend next summer here. I'm arranging for her to do an internship at the *Gazette.*"

"Is she dating anyone?"

"No one yet. Or at least, no one she's ready to tell me about."

"I'm glad she's adjusting well. Now, about you."

"Me?" I repeated.

"How are you doing?"

I took a deep breath. "Good, actually. Better than I should be. I mean, I've been through a lot this year."

Emily's gaze was sympathetic. "By any measure."

I rattled off my list. "Divorced, laid off from my job, Anna leaving for college, and then everything that's happened here in Eagle Cove the past few weeks...."

"You seem to be holding up."

"Did Claire tell you I'm reopening the cafe? Me and Janie?"

Emily smiled. "She did. I'm happy for you both. Janie is the perfect partner for you."

"Did she tell you we're keeping the name?"

Emily's eyes widened. "Emily's Eats?"

"In honor of the woman we both love and admire tremendously."

Emily teared up. "You don't have to do that."

"Already done. The new owners have made their decision and they're sticking to it."

Emily chuckled but stopped when she gasped with sudden pain.

"Are you okay?" I said anxiously.

"My ribs," Emily said. "They're still very…."

"Got it." I glanced toward Claire. "I think it's time to let you get some rest."

"One last question."

"Ask away."

"Tell me about Matt."

I went still. To be honest, I'd been hoping to avoid that particular topic. Because what was I going to say? That even after all these years, the sight of him took my breath away? That just thinking about him got me tingly and flustered? That being near him made me feel like a teenager again, which of course was ridiculous and silly and embarrassing, but also possibly really, really good?

"Matt's great," I said, trying to sound calm and measured. "He's been very helpful and supportive through all of this."

"What Sarah means," Claire said, jumping in, "is that they're still hot for each other."

My eyes narrowed. "Traitor."

"The truth shall set you free," Claire shot back.

"Girls," Emily said mildly.

I shook my head. "Even if Claire's right — and I admit nothing — the reality is that we're different people now. It's been twenty-plus years. I'm not rushing into anything."

"A wise stance for now," Emily said. "Until the current situation settles down. I've always liked Matthew. He's proven to be a fine sheriff. But it's important for him to remain out of the loop on this."

"I won't be sharing any of this spy stuff with him, I promise."

"Good." Her gaze intensified. "In every other respect, I hope you don't hold back. Should you feel the impulse to leap, I urge you to do just that."

I gulped. "Voice of experience?"

My aunt gave my hand a squeeze. "The women in our family need a man who can keep us on our toes."

Tears came. "Aunt Emily, I'm so glad you're alive."

Emily's eyes glistened. "Love is what makes life worth living. When fate offers you that chance, grab on and hold tight."

CHAPTER 6

Three months had passed since my surprise reunion with Emily in that hospital room, but I still thought about her every day. As I drove toward the lake that frigid February morning, I couldn't help but reflect again on her words of wisdom about Matt.

The truth when it came to Matt was that, despite our undeniable connection, I'd been keeping him at arm's length since moving back to Eagle Cove. I'd immersed myself in everything else going on in my life — settling into Aunt Emily's third-floor apartment, enjoying the hustle and bustle of Christmas with my family, working day and night to restart Emily's Eats — instead of opening myself to the possibility of rediscovering what we'd once had.

Because you're scared, my inner truth-teller told me. *You're afraid you'll fail. Again.*

I couldn't argue with that. My marriage had failed. The divorce had hurt me deeply. I wasn't ready for a new relationship. There were moments when I wondered whether I'd ever be ready, or even deserved to be ready.

Somehow, bless his heart, Matt seemed to understand all of that, even as he continued to make his interest in me clear. Most mornings, usually around eleven after the early rush, he stopped by the cafe for a coffee and scone to chat about normal things — safe things, regular things. But beneath the casual banter, I sensed his emotional energy, keen and raring to go, his grey eyes alive and full of feeling. The daily coffee visits were his way of checking in on me. If anything, he had a better read on my anxiety and self-doubt than I did.

With a sigh, I pulled into the marina parking lot and parked next to his truck in front of the office shack. Aside from his truck, the lakefront was deserted. The crowd from the crime scene had dispersed, almost like they'd never been here.

So where was Matt? I was reaching for my phone when I noticed a note on the door of the shack with my name on it in big letters.

I climbed out of the car and dashed to the

shack, pulling my coat tight to protect against the frigid morning air. The note was in his handwriting and said, "Join me at the ice cabin."

I sighed. He wanted me to go out there *again*?

I was about to call to suggest an alternate meeting spot — the inside of my comfy, well-heated car would do quite nicely, thank you very much — when I remembered there was no cell service on the ice. Hoping against hope, I dialed anyway and got sent straight to his voicemail.

Grrrr. Accepting the inevitable, I returned to the car for my gloves and scarf, locked up, and made my way down to the shore to the frozen lake. The air was still bitterly cold and the gusts of wind just as intense. But in the grey morning light, the walk across the ice to the cabin seemed easier, the distance shorter. The hills surrounding the lake were beautiful, the trees dusted with snow. As I approached the cabin, I noticed the shoreline near the cabin rising steeply from the water into a thick stand of pine.

After knocking loudly on the cabin door, I heard Matt yell, "Come in!"

I opened the door and found him in the kitchen area, bundled up in his heavy winter coat. He waved me in. "Sarah, thanks for coming out."

I shut the door behind me and held up the bag. "I brought your favorites."

He grinned. "Thanks."

I gave him a quick once-over as I set the bag on the dining table. His handsome face was tired and drawn — no surprise, given the night he'd had. "Have you slept?"

He shook his head. "I'll sleep tonight."

"How about your deputies?"

"Sent them home for naps."

"I heard you found two more bodies under the ice."

"You heard that from…?"

"Wendy Danvers. She came by the cafe this morning."

He grunted. "She was here most of the night."

"I take it the three dead men were friends?"

"Colleagues. Scientists at a research lab at Middlemore University."

"And I take it that what happened here was no accident?"

His eyes didn't leave mine. "What happened here was murder."

I shivered. He was being quite forthcoming. That wasn't typical. Sheriffs like him tended not to share information with nosy civilians like me. Plus, he wasn't a fan of me poking around. The last time I'd dug into a mystery, I'd nearly died.

Yet here I was, at his request.

"Tell me how I can help," I said.

"I'm hoping a return to the scene might jog loose additional details."

That wasn't his real reason for asking me back here, but I let the explanation pass. "Worth a shot." I glanced toward the ice hole in the center of the cabin floor, ignoring a surge of queasiness as I flashed to the unseeing eyes of Howard, the dead man I'd reeled in.

"Anything look out of place?" he asked.

I circled slowly, absorbing details as I went. Aside from the basics, I hadn't paid much attention to the cabin's interior during my previous visit. But now I noticed that the place looked pretty modern. Aside from the missing floor, the decor was clean and fresh. The small dining table and four chairs were solid oak. The small kitchenette boasted a granite countertop and cherry cabinets and was equipped with a small sink, small fridge, microwave oven, and stovetop grill.

"It's nicer than I would have thought," I said.

"Ice Cabin 2.0."

I continued my survey of the space. "Some of the stuff that was here last night isn't here now."

"What stuff?"

"The fishing poles, for one."

"At the lab for analysis."

"There was a bag of takeout food, too. From the Golden Dragon. Unopened."

"Also at the lab. Anything else?"

I found myself frowning at the boot print on the ice near the dining table. "I noticed this print last night."

"What did you notice about it?"

I paused, staring hard at the dark brown pattern on the grey ice, trying to recall. "Only that it was here. Don't tell me it's blood."

"It's blood."

"So someone stepped in blood and then…." I realized I was frowning. "It doesn't make sense."

"What doesn't?"

"The boot that left the bloody print had to step in blood. When I got here, I didn't see any blood."

His eyes held mine. "What do you make of that?"

"Are you saying you didn't find any other blood here in the ice cabin?"

"No visible blood, no."

"So…." I realized what he was telling me. "The killer cleaned up the rest of the cabin but missed the bloody boot print."

"Perhaps."

"Or?"

"Or left it on purpose."

I blinked, startled. "Why would he do that?"

Matt took a long breath, then pointed to the ice floor in the kitchenette. "Tell me what you think of that."

I pivoted and leaned closer for a better look.

The icy floor in front of the kitchen sink appeared to have a scar in it, a white slash in the grey ice. The scar was square-shaped and easily a good three feet wide.

"It looks like someone cut into the ice here."

"*Through* the ice, actually."

I glanced at him. "Through?"

"There was a second hole — a bigger hole, about three feet square — here in the kitchen area. It appears the killer was doing something under the ice."

I frowned and stepped closer. "You're saying a big hole was cut here and the block of ice was removed and then…."

"Later on, when the hole was no longer needed, the block of ice was put back into the hole to seal it back up."

I tried to wrap my head around that. Was that how the killer had gained entry? Had he cut a hole in the ice floor to slip into the cabin?

Don't be silly, I told myself. The idea of someone sneaking into the cabin from below was totally James Bond-ish — ridiculous, in other words. I tried to imagine the killer, clad in wetsuit and scuba gear, armed with a fancy high-tech waterproof hacksaw or maybe a superheated knife or even a top-secret laser weapon, stealthily approaching the cabin from below and slicing silently through a foot of thick ice to slip in undetected….

"I don't get how that would work," I said. "How does one even do that?"

He shrugged. "Cutting a hole in ice isn't difficult. Basically, you pick a spot and start boring or sawing."

"Wouldn't the men have heard the sawing or drilling or whatever?"

"If they were conscious and awake, most likely yes."

I paused as I absorbed his words. Matt had a way of telling me stuff without telling me.

"Do we know if the victims were unconscious prior to the killer's arrival?" I asked carefully.

"We'll know more when the blood work comes back."

"You suspect the victims were ... drugged?"

He shrugged. "Boring or sawing a hole through the ice isn't a silent endeavor."

"So if the victims were awake, they would have heard it."

"Most likely, yes." His eyes were fixed on me, like he was waiting for me to catch up.

"Maybe they all got really drunk and passed out? I mean, isn't that the point of this ice-fishing nonsense — an excuse for grown men to escape the civilizing influence of women and get thoroughly plastered?"

That won me a smile. "Not a fan of ice fishing, I see."

"Consider me a skeptic."

"You should give it a try. It's not all about drinking and male misbehaving."

"Really?"

"It can be a contemplative experience." He seemed sincere as he said it. "A chance to get away from the pressures of daily life, reconnect with nature, bond with friends and family."

I flashed to his two sons, a junior and a freshman in high school.

"Your boys like it, I take it?"

"We've spent a weekend on the ice every winter since moving here."

"Do they enjoy it?"

"They didn't at first. Their phones don't work out here — no signal."

My eyes widened. "No texting? Teenage catastrophe."

He chuckled. "After the complaining died down and they put their phones away, they started getting into it."

"You catch any fish?"

"Sure. The lake is full of trout and pike."

"And you … eat them?"

He pointed to the stovetop. "Grill 'em right there.""

"The men who rented the cabin this weekend didn't have much confidence in their fishing skills."

"Why do you say that?"

"They ordered delivery."

The observation pleased him, I could tell. He was enjoying talking through this with me.

I had a flash of insight. "Maybe the three men were expecting the killer."

"That's certainly possible, yes."

"Any idea who the killer was, or the motive?"

"Not yet, no."

"Maybe the three men cut the bigger hole themselves."

"Possibly, yes."

"Did you find any equipment for that in the cabin?"

He shook his head. "The killer may have taken it with him or…."

"Or dumped it in the lake."

"We're bringing in a dive team to conduct an underwater search."

"If we accept that the men cut the big hole themselves, do we also believe the men knew their killer?"

"That's what I believe, yes."

"Maybe the killer even helped them cut the hole in the ice?"

"Quite possibly."

"You seem pretty sure about the killer having a connection to the three men."

He exhaled slowly, his eyes not leaving mine. "What I'm about to tell you, I'm telling you for two reasons. One, I know you can keep a secret."

"Oh, you know that about me, do you?"

"I do."

His gaze was steady as he allowed the silence to linger. He wasn't wrong. Once I knew a secret, I was good at keeping it. I pushed back a twinge of guilt about everything I was keeping from him about Claire, Aunt Emily, and the secret spy world they inhabited.

I broke the silence. "What's the other reason?"

"The other reason — the main reason, to be honest — is that I want you to *not* feel the urge to poke around for answers yourself."

"No nosy Sarah?"

"Not this time. Not with this case. You need to stay away from this one. I'm saying this with complete seriousness."

The ease and flow of our conversation had vanished. Whatever Matt was about to share troubled him.

"Tell me what you're worried about."

He took another deep breath.

"Matt, tell me."

"The hooks," he finally said.

"You mean, the hooks from the fishing lines that the bodies got snagged on?"

"'Snagged on' isn't accurate."

I frowned, confused. "What do you mean?"

"The hooks were applied deliberately. Post-mortem."

A second wave of queasiness rolled through me. I'd thought I'd figured out how everything had gone down, but that detail didn't fit — at all.

"But wait. How is that possible?"

"It's why we know scuba equipment was involved."

"Okay, hang on," I said, totally not following. "Let me walk through this."

"Sure."

"The killer murdered the three men here in the cabin."

"Right."

"Then he pushed the bodies into the water through the big square ice hole in the kitchen floor...."

"Right."

"And you're saying the bodies didn't just drift and get tangled in the fishing lines and get hooked by chance?"

"Right."

"You're saying the fishing hooks were attached to the bodies *deliberately*?"

"Correct."

"How?"

"The only way they could have been."

"I'm not with you yet." I looked around the cabin, trying to figure it out. I walked over to the small ice hole in the living area between the two facing couches. The hole was barely a foot wide — definitely too small to stuff a body through. "The three fishing poles were set up here. The lines fed through the small hole into the water."

"Right."

I glanced toward the kitchen floor. "You're saying the killer got into the water himself and went under the ice and … hooked each body to a fishing line?"

"Correct."

"Using scuba equipment?"

"Almost certainly, yes."

"But why?" I whispered, thoroughly baffled.

The conflict playing across Matt's face filled me with sudden dread.

"Sarah," he said, his tone conveying his uncertainty. "What I'm about to tell you — you have to promise not to say a word to anyone."

"Of course."

His eyes drilled into me.

"Not a peep. Promise."

His jaw clenched.

"Matt, tell me."

He exhaled. "The hooks were attached in three specific ways."

I breathed in sharply. My imagination ran riot. Fear jolted me. The thing is, I abhor violence. I hate horror movies. I cover my eyes during the scary parts. Seeing blood or gore on TV or in movies nearly always grosses me out.

Did I really want to know the specifics of this crime?

Did I?

Apparently the answer was yes, because I heard myself whispering, "Tell me how."

Matt took another breath and then said, his voice deliberately straightforward and level, "One victim had a hook attached to his ear, one had a hook attached to his eyebrow, and one had a hook attached to his lip."

I went still as his words sank in. "No way that happened by chance."

He shook his head. "No way."

A flash of insight mixed with horror shot through me. "The killer was sending a message."

"Most definitely."

"'Hear no evil, see no evil, speak no evil.'"

His gaze intensified. "Now that you know, Sarah, I'm holding you to your promise."

"Of course," I whispered.

"Not a word to anyone."

"Of course."

"Furthermore, you're going to steer clear of this one. No digging around. No searching for the truth. No pursuing justice."

"Of course," I repeated a third time, realizing

as the words left my mouth that this time, I was actually telling him the truth.

Whatever was going on here had nothing to do with me. This killer was ruthless. And twisted. He had an agenda.

I shivered. This was one mystery I had no desire to solve.

CHAPTER 7

We didn't stick around long after that. Matt was tired and had a busy day ahead of him, and I was eager to leave the ice cabin, hopefully never to return. He walked me across the ice to my car and waved goodbye as I headed out. Through the rear-view mirror, I saw him watching me as I rounded the bend and vanished into the trees.

On the short drive back to the cafe, I tried to organize my thoughts — no easy task, given everything I'd learned.

Matt had shared a lot, which I appreciated. But so much remained unknown.

Had he identified a suspect? Not yet.

Had he identified a motive? Not yet.

Had he determined the means? Yes, at least

probably. His working theory made sense. The forensics would either confirm his suspicions or not.

I realized there was probably stuff he hadn't told me. His goal in bringing me to the ice cabin was to keep me from nosing around — to satiate my insatiable curiosity, to quell my natural instinct to poke and pry. To achieve that goal, he'd shared exactly what he felt he needed to, and he'd been crystal-clear and aboveboard about doing that.

So I had no reasonable grounds for being irritated with him. Still, I felt a stirring of annoyance — and interest — as I wondered what he hadn't shared.

On Main Street, I eased into a parking spot across the street from Emily's Eats and turned my attention to a more immediate issue: what to tell the gang in the cafe. Between Gabby prodding and Mr. Benson inquiring and Mom worrying, I was about to walk into a minefield. The instant I set foot inside, a savvy team of small-town information-retrieval specialists would swarm me and interrogate me to within an inch of my life. My every word, my every tone, my every pause would be consumed and digested and analyzed. If any of them sensed me holding back, I was doomed.

I took a deep breath. Aside from the hooks, was there anything I needed to withhold?

No, I concluded as I gazed across the street at the cafe that had become the center of my existence. Through the big front windows, I saw Mom ringing up a customer at the register and Janie setting a freshly baked pie in the display case. Mr. Benson was on his stool at the counter, reading a newspaper. Hialeah was at her usual table by the window, sipping a cup of tea. Though I couldn't see Gabby in her booth, it was safe to assume she was there as well.

I got out of the car, squared my shoulders, and made my way across the street. The second I pushed open the cafe door, all movement and conversation ceased. Mom looked up from the register, relief and alarm playing across her face. Janie shot a warning glance toward Gabby's booth.

"Is that her?" Gabby yelled. A second later, my octogenarian neighbor barreled out of the booth and rushed me, cane waving wildly in front of her.

"Gabby," I said, retreating a step and preparing for the worst. "What's going on?"

"What kept you? We've been waiting."

"Waiting for what?"

"For you!"

"I told you I wouldn't be long, and I promised I'd share all when I returned."

"Bah!" She seemed more agitated than usual. "Not that."

"Then what?"

"You need to save Tony!"

I blinked with confusion.

Who was Tony?

"Before the killers get him!"

Killers?

"Gabby…."

"Don't you 'Gabby' me. This is serious." Concern cracked through her pushy exterior. Her eyes flashed worry — even a hint of panic.

Grabbing my arm, she dragged me to the booth, where I saw that one of Gabby's fellow octogenarians, Mrs. Chan, had joined us.

"Ellie," Gabby said to Mrs. Chan. "Tell Sarah."

When Mrs. Chan looked up at me, I saw mascara smudges under her eyes. She'd been crying. A tiny woman who dressed elegantly and conservatively, Mrs. Chan had a careful manner that blossomed into cheerful good humor when she relaxed. Her laugh, high and loud, had a way of rising above the booth and bringing a smile to my lips whenever I heard it.

But there was no laughter this morning. "It's my grandson, Tony," she said. "He didn't come home last night."

Fear shot through me as I began connecting dots. Mrs. Chan's family owned the Golden Dragon restaurant. The restaurant did a lot of delivery. Last night at the ice cabin, I'd seen a bag of takeout food from the Golden Dragon.

"A sheriff's deputy called this morning and said our delivery truck is in the impound lot," Mrs.

Chan continued, her voice trembling. "They asked if we did any deliveries last night."

"What did you tell them?"

"I said I would check and call them back."

"What did you do then?"

Her eyebrows rose. "I came right here."

"Why?"

Her eyes filled with tears. "Because we have to find Tony!"

Gabby stepped closer. "Sarah, what's gotten into you?"

"What do you mean?"

"I thought you were smart."

"Wait," I said, not following.

"Tony didn't come home last night," Mrs. Chan said.

Ah. The dots were connecting. "He was doing deliveries for the restaurant?"

When she nodded, I tried to keep my face and tone neutral. "I see."

"What did the sheriff tell you?" Gabby demanded.

"He didn't say anything about Tony."

Mr. Benson cleared his throat. "But you know something, don't you, Sarah?"

"It's just...." I paused to figure out the right words, my mind racing. Did I dare continue? Yes, my gut told me — it was better for the facts to be known. "When I went to the lake last night, I saw a truck parked in the marina lot. I'm not sure, but I'm guessing the truck was Tony's."

"Oh, no," Mrs. Chan said.

"And last night, inside the ice cabin, I saw takeout from the Golden Dragon. A big bag, unopened."

Mrs. Chan gasped. "Tony was there!"

"Not necessarily," I said immediately. "The men might have met Tony on shore and brought the food to the ice cabin themselves."

Except there's no cell service on the lake, I didn't add.

"But if he wasn't there, then where is he?" Mrs. Chan cried.

It was an excellent question, but unanswerable. I pushed back a surge of dread, the anguish in Mrs. Chan's voice painful to hear.

"We're going to figure that out." I steeled myself — it was time to step up and channel my inner Aunt Emily. "This will be a team effort. Is everyone on board?"

Six heads — Mrs. Chan, Gabby, Mr. Benson, Mom, Janie, and Hialeah — bobbed in quick assent.

"Mrs. Chan, we need you to write down a list of all of Tony's friends and all of the places he likes to hang out. The list should include everyone and anyone he might call or places he might go if he needed help. We're going to call every single person on that list.

"The rest of you, I want you to reach out to everyone you know and ask if they've seen Tony, either today or yesterday. Keep notes of who you talked to and what they said. And be sure to call everyone, because you never know."

I swiveled to Mom. "Can you get hold of Betsy and find out everything you can?"

Mom nodded and I turned to Janie. "I need to call Matt again. I'll do it upstairs. Can I ask you to…?"

"Of course," Janie said. "We'll manage here fine. I'll call if we hear anything."

"Thanks. Back in a few."

At the door leading to the hallway, I paused and gazed at the six of them — each so different from the others in so many ways — uniting around a common goal.

The lump in my throat shouldn't have taken me by surprise, but it did.

With effort, I switched my attention to the task I'd assigned myself. Matt hadn't shared a peep about Tony and the Golden Dragon. Now he was going to, whether he wanted to or not.

Stepping into the hallway, I firmly shut the cafe door behind me and headed toward the stairs.

That's when I heard it — a sound.

Of *footsteps*. Behind me.

My heart leaped into my throat.

I wasn't alone in the hallway!

CHAPTER 8

I whirled, heart racing, and found myself staring at—

A kid.

A *scared* kid.

He was about sixteen and Asian, with short, straight black hair and anxious dark eyes, dressed in a winter coat, boots, and jeans. A few inches taller than me, he looked thin and young beneath his heavy blue coat.

In his eyes was a mixture of wariness and jumpiness and, yes, *fear*.

"You're Tony, right?" I said, hoping against hope that I was right. "Tony Chan?"

He gave me a quick nod, his gaze darting to the cafe door.

"I'm so glad you're safe."

He gestured to the door. "Can they hear us talking?"

"No," I said, taken aback. "Why do you ask?"

"You're the lady who owns the cafe, right?" His voice was clear but nervous.

"I am."

"You're Claire's friend?"

I blinked, going on high alert. Why was he bringing up *Claire*?

"Yes," I said cautiously. "Claire is a friend of mine."

Tony swallowed and stared hard at me, as if making a big decision. I noticed he was holding something — a small box, perhaps — wrapped in a plastic garbage bag. "Okay," he said, as much to himself as to me. "Okay."

"Tony," I said, "what's going on?"

"Can we go someplace quiet?"

"Of course. But first, how about we let your family know you're safe?" I gestured to the cafe door. "Your grandmother's here. She's worried sick about you."

"No," he said immediately. "No way. You can't. Not yet."

"Tony, I think we should —"

"No." He edged toward the hallway entry door, as if preparing to flee.

"Okay," I said quickly. "Tony, we'll do it your way. We'll go to a quiet place to talk."

"Where?" he said suspiciously.

"I live upstairs. Top floor. We can head right up."

After a short pause, he said, "You go first."

"Okay." As I turned toward the stairs, the thought came: Tony was acting like a scared kid, but what if he wasn't? How deeply involved in the murders was he?

Was it possible I was walking upstairs with a killer?

I climbed slowly, keeping my pace measured and calm. Worrying about this young man was silly, I tried to reassure myself. I had no reason to believe he was anything other than a good kid, a regular kid. I would have heard if he weren't. Right now, he seemed scared and uncertain. That was all.

My gut didn't object to that argument, so I took a deep breath and continued climbing.

At the last flight of stairs, I glanced over my shoulder. "My name is Sarah."

"Grandma mentioned you," Tony said. "She said you cracked the case of who killed the plumber guy."

I flashed to poor Jerry, murdered in my basement because he recognized the wrong person at the wrong time, and again I felt a rush of guilt. For the millionth time, I wished I'd pieced the clues together sooner.

"How do you know Claire?" I said.

"I don't."

I almost stopped right there — *his answer made no sense* — but kept going. The kid was clearly on edge. He needed to feel safe.

After reaching the third floor, I opened the apartment door and ushered him in. My aunt had lived in this spacious, sunny, top-floor unit for thirty years, and I'd always loved its gracious rooms, high ceilings, and well-curated mix of original artwork and midcentury and antique furnishings. Though I'd had vague ambitions about switching things up when I moved in, I'd quickly realized that Aunt Emily's decorating choices suited me perfectly. Aside from adding a few family photos, I hadn't changed a thing.

As Tony made his way into the living room, his gaze was drawn to the long wall covered with Emily's travel photos. For more than twenty years, Aunt Emily and Uncle Ted had crisscrossed the globe and snapped photos wherever they landed. Until a few months ago, I'd believed their travels were for Ted's job with an oil company. Now I knew that the two of them, husband and wife, had been spies.

Tony stepped closer to the photos for a better look. I switched on the table lamp next to the sofa and waited.

"I knew her," he said. "Emily, I mean. Was she your aunt?"

"Great-aunt, actually. My mother's aunt."

"How old was she when she died?"

You mean when she pretended to die, I didn't say. "Eighty-three."

"I had to help set up the Flower Festival," he said, referring to the big flower show that Eagle Cove hosted each spring. "She was running the committee." He glanced toward me. "Cool lady. Totally in charge, but nice about it, you know? I'm sorry for your loss."

"Thank you," I said, touched by his words. I found myself warming to him. Whatever his flaws might be — he was a teenager, after all — he was coming across as respectful and thoughtful.

He pointed to a photo of Emily and Ted in front of the Trevi fountain in Rome. The photo was probably forty years old. Emily's hair was dark brown and her skin was wrinkle-free, but her thin, angular face and vivid grey eyes were unmistakable. "Where's this one?"

"Rome."

His eyes widened. "You mean like gladiators and togas?"

I smiled. "That's right."

"I'm gonna travel someday. As soon as I graduate, I'm outta here."

"Eagle Cove isn't where you want to stay?"

He shook his head. "Too small."

I felt a pang — of nostalgia, of regret — at his words. I'd felt much the same when I was his age.

"Are you aiming for college?"

"That's what my parents and Grandma want."

"You're a junior in high school?"

He nodded, his gaze still on the photos. For the next few moments, he asked about different locations — London, Paris, Hong Kong, Tokyo, Beijing — before finally returning his attention to me.

"Let me get you something to drink," I said.

"What do you have?"

After running through the options, we agreed on Earl Grey tea and I urged him to take a seat in the living room. As the water boiled, I asked him about himself and his family. His parents had opened the restaurant before he was born, he told me. His younger sister was twelve. His grandma — who I knew as Mrs. Chan — had moved here from New York four years ago, after his grandpa died.

He was on the varsity track team and liked it, and played the trumpet in the school band but wasn't into it. He wasn't exactly talkative, but he was willing to answer my questions, so I kept asking. I sensed he was still mostly a kid, though soon enough he'd be graduating to young adulthood.

I brought a teapot, sugar, milk, two mugs, and two spoons into the living room, then set everything on the coffee table in front of the sofa he'd chosen to sit on. I settled into a side chair. "How do you like your tea? Sugar? Milk?"

"Lots of sugar," he said immediately.

I poured him a cup and gestured to a spoon. "Add however much you want."

"Thanks."

I was about to turn the conversation to the pressing matter at hand when I heard a familiar scratching sound from the kitchen. I turned and saw Mr. Snuggles, my curious and confident tabby pal, emerge from the old dumbwaiter shaft in the kitchen wall. With athletic ease, he dashed into the living room and, without hesitation, leaped onto the couch beside Tony.

"Who's this?" Tony said, a smile lighting up his face.

"Meet Mr. Snuggles," I replied.

My feline friend regarded Tony carefully, giving him a thorough inspection.

"He's a big guy," Tony said, cautiously extending his hand.

Choosing to investigate further, Mr. Snuggles inched forward and rubbed his face against Tony's hand. Then, almost before we could blink, he clambered onto Tony's stomach and started rubbing himself against his chest, purring loudly.

"Wow, he's so friendly," Tony said with a gasp.

"When he wants to be."

"Okay if I pet him?"

"That's up to him. He'll let you know."

I watched as the two of them got comfortable with each other.

"How old is he?" Tony asked.

"About five."

"I take it he's yours?"

"He's more like everyone's."

He looked up at me. "Everyone's?"

"Mr. Snuggles has the run of the building, top floor to basement." I gestured toward the kitchen. "There's an old dumbwaiter shaft that he uses to climb up and down."

Tony's eyes widened. "Up and down the entire building?"

"Mr. Benson and Gabby McBride — they live in apartments on the second floor — also take care of him."

Tony regarded Mr. Snuggles fondly. "I wish I had a cat."

"Maybe someday you will." I felt an itch of impatience — Mr. Snuggles wasn't the only curious creature in the room — but brushed the feeling aside. "Before we start, can I get you anything to eat?"

He shook his head. "I had a box of cereal earlier."

I realized he'd said *box* and not *bowl*. "An entire box?"

"It was all that was there," he began, then

stopped, as if worrying he'd said something he shouldn't have.

"Well, if you change your mind, let me know," I replied, choosing for the moment not to push. "I can make you a sandwich if you'd like."

His gaze stayed on me for a few long seconds — I was being evaluated. "I guess you want to know what happened."

"I do," I said, my heart beating faster. "Start wherever you'd like."

CHAPTER 9

Tony glanced down at Mr. Snuggles — who had apparently decided that Tony's lap was the perfect place for a nap — before returning his attention to me. "Can I ask you a question?"

"Of course."

"The radio said the sheriff found *three* dead guys in the ice cabin?"

"Yes, that's right."

The information seemed to bother him. He chewed on it for a few seconds. "You're friends with the sheriff, right?"

"Yes, he's a friend."

His tone was wary. "Does he think I did it?"

"Oh, no," I said immediately, even as I realized that I didn't know that for sure.

"But he found my truck there."

"Right."

"And he towed it to the impound yard."

"And you know that because…?"

"I saw them towing it when I was coming here."

"The sheriff will want to talk with you," I said carefully. "But I expect as a witness. He'll want to know what you saw yesterday."

"Yeah," Tony said, still not convinced. "Okay."

Fear flashed through his eyes.

"Tony," I said calmly but firmly, trying to channel my inner Aunt Emily. "I can put in a good word for you. And I will do that for you, I promise. Now, tell me what happened."

"Okay." From his tone, I sensed he was finally ready to share. "I went there because they called in an order."

I smiled encouragingly, realizing I'd have to help him unpack his story. "The victims called your restaurant?"

"Right."

"To order delivery?"

"Right."

"Who called in the order?"

"The guy in the ice cabin."

"He called in — when?"

"Yesterday morning. He said he was going ice fishing with his buddies and wanted dinner delivered to the ice cabin at six."

I nodded. The victim I'd met, Howard

Penn, had done much the same when he'd ordered muffins at the cafe.

"He told me which cabin and what he wanted, and I told him we'd be there at six."

"You took the order?"

"Yeah."

"Okay, tell me what happened next."

"Nothing," he said. "At least, not till dinnertime. Then we got the order together and I got in the truck and drove to the lake."

Mr. Snuggles seemed to sense Tony's tension. He rolled onto his back and gazed up at Tony's face, almost as if expressing silent support.

"Do you deliver food to the ice cabins often?"

"Usually Dad does the deliveries. But I have my driver's license now and he's sick at home — the flu — so last night I did it."

"Okay," I said, struck again by how young he was. "You got to the lake, and then...."

"I took the order there. It's a long walk across the ice from where you park, but anyway, I got to the ice cabin and knocked on the door and didn't hear anything, so I knocked again and tried the door and the door opened and I went in and —"

He stopped, as if stricken.

"You're doing great, Tony. You went in and...."

"I saw a guy on the ground, with a spear — a spear! — through him."

My eyes widened. "A *spear*?"

"Yeah, a spear. From a speargun."

"What did you do then?"

"I thought he was dead. I got closer and was checking for a pulse when he reached up and grabbed at me."

"He was still alive?" I gasped.

"He was like, 'Who are you?' Wild-eyed,' you know? I said I was the delivery guy and he fell back and kind of groaned — like he was disappointed? — and said, 'Where is he?'"

"Did he mean, where's the killer?"

"I think so. And I was like, 'Who are you talking about?' and he said, 'Where's the box?'"

"The box?" I said, my eyes darting to the object in the garbage bag at his feet, which I'd almost forgotten about.

"He pointed to it and said I had to take it and run. And I was like, 'I need to call an ambulance for you,' and he's like, 'He'll be back any minute. You can't let him get it. Take it and run!'"

I couldn't believe what I was hearing — and yet I believed him completely.

"And then?"

Tony's breath quickened. "I heard a sound behind me and turned and saw a dude in a wetsuit coming up through a hole in the ice."

I inhaled sharply. *A dude in a wetsuit?* It really was like a spy movie. "And then?"

"He had a speargun and he aimed it at me and fired."

I gasped. "Did he hit you? Are you hurt?"

"He missed, barely. The spear *whooshed* by my head. Then the dude yelled 'Don't move!' and started climbing out of the ice hole and slipped and fell back in."

"And then?"

"The guy on the ground next to me — the guy with the spear in him, the one I thought was dead? — grabbed my foot and said, 'Take the box to Claire's friend at the cafe. She'll know what to do.'"

I gaped at him, stunned. "He said *what*?"

"So when the guy grabbed my foot, it jolted me, you know? Before I knew it, I grabbed the box and tore out of there. The wetsuit dude tried to stop me but he slipped on the ice again and I got out of the cabin and I just *took off*. I'm on the track team, okay? But getting across the ice was like a mad scramble."

"Tony," I said, still barely able to process what I'd heard. Not only had the victim mentioned me, but he'd referred to me as *Claire's friend at the cafe*? "I'm so glad you got away."

"Me, too." He exhaled deeply. "Me, too."

I wanted him to elaborate on what he'd just told me — the urge was nearly irresistible — but he was clearly in the flow of his story, so instead I said, "What did you do then?"

"I started toward my truck, but it was parked really far away — way across the ice — so I aimed for the closest part of the shore so I could get to the trees. It's a good thing, too, because the wetsuit dude? He came racing out of the cabin after me with a real gun. I'd just reached shore and ducked behind a tree when he started firing."

"Did he chase after you?"

"Totally. I just kept climbing up the ridge. I know the woods pretty well, so once I got in the trees, I knew he wouldn't get me."

I nodded, relating to his confidence. Local kids like Tony (and me) knew the woods near the lake like the backs of our hands.

"Did he give up?"

"He was still in his wetsuit and he didn't have on real boots — just, like, wetsuit shoes, you know? — and it's so cold out. He kept at it a while, but he had to give up. Dressed the way he was, he didn't have a choice."

"When he gave up, he…."

"He went back to the cabin. I watched from the woods, trying to decide if I should make a run for my truck. After about fifteen minutes, I saw him come out, dressed in regular clothes and carrying a bunch of gear across the ice to the parking lot. He brought everything to his truck — I mean, I'm guessing it was his truck — and loaded it in the back."

"And then?"

Fear returned to Tony's eyes. "He saw my truck and went over and checked it out and snapped a photo of the license plate and the side door."

I went still. "Your truck has a sign for the restaurant painted on the side door?"

"Golden Dragon Restaurant. Address, phone, website — all of it."

"What did he do then?"

"He reached behind the front tire and did something."

I realized immediately what the killer had done, but I didn't want to alarm him. "And by something, you mean…?"

"He put a GPS tracker on the truck." He stated it like it was obvious, then shot me a doubtful look — like he'd expected more from me and was worried he'd made a mistake coming here.

"Tony," I said, trying to allay his unspoken concern. "I'm on the same page. Are you saying you didn't go back to your truck after he left?"

He shook his head. "No way. You think I'm gonna let him track me? What went down — it's like something out of the movies. That dude is scary."

"So after the wetsuit dude" — I heard myself using his term — "put the tracker on your truck, what did he do?"

"He got in his truck and drove north."

"Have you seen him since?"

He shook his head and I saw another flash of fear. As brave and resourceful as Tony was, inside he was still a scared kid.

"After he drove away, what did you do?"

He shrugged. "For a while, not much. I kind of just sat there and thought about what to do."

"Did you call anyone?"

He shook his head. "I left my phone in the truck when I brought the food to the cabin."

"When you left the woods, where did you go?"

He tensed, and I knew he didn't want to tell me.

"Tony, I promise I won't tell anyone."

He looked at me keenly but stayed silent.

"I grew up in Eagle Cove, too," I said softly. "I know what it's like to be a teenager in this town. A town full of vacation homes, many of them empty this time of year…."

His eyes flashed with appreciation. "Maybe what you're thinking is maybe what I did."

"Anything broken or damaged getting in?"

"Maybe the owner leaves the key under the flower pot by the front door."

I gave him a conspiratorial smile. "How's the heating?"

That got me a grin. "Maybe it's pretty good."

"And the entertainment system?"

"Maybe it's a totally rad gaming setup."

"Did you clean up after yourself?"

"Maybe we always leave it the way we found it."

I ignored the *we* — clearly, playing video games at this unoccupied lake house was a group activity. "So that's where you slept?"

"On the couch, maybe."

"The box of cereal?"

"It's all that was there. I'll replace it later."

"Did you make any calls?"

"I stopped at the gas station last night and called Grandma and told her the truck wouldn't start and I was staying the night with a friend."

"And she said...."

He sighed. "She knew I was lying. She called me irresponsible and said I needed to get back to the restaurant to make deliveries because I have a duty to support the family."

"And you said...?"

He looked at me guiltily. "I mean, she's not wrong, but what could I say? 'Sorry, Grandma, no deliveries tonight. I'm on the run from a secret agent who just murdered a guy and tried to kill me.'"

I went still, not sure what I'd just heard. "Secret agent?"

"Yeah," he said matter-of-factly.

"You know that because...."

"Because of the guys who got killed."

I blinked, totally not following. "You know them?"

"Well, it's not like I *know* them. But they come to the restaurant sometimes. Lately, they've been coming a lot. The guy who got speared? His name is Howard."

I flashed to the face I'd seen exactly twice — the first time in my cafe, cheerful and alive, ordering muffins for delivery, and the second time in the ice hole, cold and dead, a fishing hook imbedded in his lip.

"Bearded guy, forties, talkative?"

He nodded. "He always did the ordering. The others were quieter. They were kind of … intense."

"So why did you say the killer is a secret agent?"

"Because they all work for the government. You know, working on secret stuff that secret agents are interested in."

"Wait," I said, still not with him. "Where did they all work?"

"At the secret government lab," he said, seemingly surprised I didn't already know.

I tried to ignore the rush of excitement at his words. "Tony, I've been away from Eagle Cove a long time. I only moved back a few months ago. You need to catch me up."

He sighed. "My friend Alice's friend Sally's mom works there. It's supposed to be all hush-hush, but everybody knows."

Everybody in your high-school crowd, I thought. *But not this clueless cafe owner.*

"What place is this?"

"Just outside Middlemore. Next to the state park. They tell people they're part of the university, but everybody knows that's a crock."

Not everyone, I thought, marveling at this town's ability to sniff out secrets.

"Anyway, they worked there."

"They told you that?"

"That Howard guy told Grandma. She likes to chat up new customers — says it's good for business."

"Tony," I said, trying to keep my tone calm, "do you think you'd recognize the wetsuit dude if you saw him again?"

He frowned. "Maybe," he finally said. "I'm not sure."

"Tell me what you noticed about him."

"White dude, stocky, tall, dark beard," he began. "He moved pretty well for a guy his size."

"Did you see his face?"

He shook his head. "He was wearing a scuba mask."

"How about in the woods?"

Another shake. "It was too dark. He never got close enough for a good look."

"You've been through a lot. I'm glad you made it out of that cabin alive."

He looked at me with a gaze that seemed calmer now, more trusting. "So … what next?"

I glanced at the object at Tony's side. "Let's talk about what's in the garbage bag."

He picked it up and handed it to me with a look of relief, like he was happy to be rid of it. After slipping off the plastic bag, I found it was a metal box — made of steel or lead, if I had to guess — and very solidly built. The edges had reinforced plating, giving it an ornate, impregnable appearance.

The top of the box was a lid with an old-fashioned keyhole lock, like the kind you find in antique writing desks.

I moved the box closer to the light for a better look. "Did you try to open it?"

"A little bit. But not really. I thought about what the wetsuit dude did to get it and I figured…."

"You figured it's best not to know."

He nodded simply.

I set the box down on the coffee table and picked up the teapot. "Refill?"

"Yes, please."

After pouring, I watched him dump in a huge spoonful of sugar — ugh, teenagers and their love of everything sweet — and stir it in.

"So let's talk about next steps," I said.

He brought the cup to his lips and looked at me gratefully, even hopefully. He'd decided to trust me, I realized. He was going to let me figure out, or at least suggest, what would happen next.

"My first concern is your safety," I began.

"And my family's," he added. "The dude knows who and where they are."

I'd been hoping he hadn't realized that, but of course he was right. "I agree."

I paused, trying to sort through my choices.

The easiest option was to call Matt right away and hand everything over to him. The sheriff's department had far more resources than I did to protect Tony and his family.

The main problem with that easy option was *Claire.* I'd promised to keep her spy job a secret. If Tony told Matt what the dead man had said — *take the box to Claire's friend at the cafe* — then Matt would know that Claire knew the victims. Inevitably, Matt would tie Claire to the hush-hush government lab near Middlemore.

The dying man's last words would also prove that I was involved in Claire's secret spy world. And when it came to Claire, Matt already suspected I was holding back.

I pushed away a rush of anxiety. The problem with Matt was that he was way too sharp and observant. He knew something was going on in our small New England town, bubbling beneath the surface. All he lacked was proof.

If I handed over the box, and if Tony told him what the dying man said, then Matt would have the evidence he needed to confirm his suspicions.

And if he used that proof to dig deeper into the larger mystery….

Claire's spy agency would not be pleased.

And don't forget Emily, I reminded myself. *If Matt discovers she's still alive*—

"Tony," I said, "I have a plan." I sat up straighter. To pull this off, I would need to come across as forthright, firm, and convincing.

Mug of tea in hand, Tony waited for me to continue.

I fixed him with an expression that I hoped was serious and reassuring. "This plan will require your complete cooperation."

"What's the plan?"

"Here's what we need to do."

CHAPTER 10

There's probably a best-practices method for teaching a teenager how to lie to law enforcement successfully — a time-tested technique written down in a book somewhere, available for would-be police deceivers like me.

That morning in the apartment, I found myself wishing I had that book. Because *How to Fool the Cops and Get Away with It* would have come in handy.

Alas, I had only my instincts to rely on. As Tony and I walked through the scheme I was proposing, I shuddered at the chance I was taking. Just as Tony was choosing to trust me, I was putting my faith in him.

If Matt ever found out what I was trying to pull off, I'd be in deep trouble. Though I was no lawyer, I'd read enough books and watched enough TV to know that "interfering with a crime scene" was a criminal charge, as was "tampering with a witness" and "withholding evidence."

But I had no better option, or at least none I could think of. The best way to get Tony and his family out of harm's way and also protect Claire's secret was to follow the plan I carefully laid out. Tony and I spent the next hour going over it, including a practice question-and-answer session to help him prepare.

Because if Matt caught even a whiff of what Tony wasn't telling him....

I gazed at the young man I was taking a leap with. He seemed calm now, even steady. The practice had been helpful for him, I sensed.

"Ready?" I said.

"Let's do it."

I picked up my phone and dialed Claire. As part of the effort to restart our frayed friendship, we'd taken to speaking regularly, or at least trying to. Half the time when I called, I was sent straight to voicemail. Usually she got back to me quickly, but on a couple of occasions, it had taken her several days to return my calls. As much as I wanted to know where she was and what she was up to — some kind of secret mission, perhaps? — so far I'd managed to refrain from asking.

I was again sent to voicemail. "Hey, it's me. You've probably heard the news up here. Well, I got my hands on something related, and I think you'll want to see it."

When I hung up, Tony nodded approvingly. "Very cryptic."

I shrugged, trying not to show that his comment pleased me. This spy stuff was rather fascinating, to be honest. Baffling, too, but undeniably exciting and exotic.

"One more call." I dialed Janie downstairs and she picked up on the first ring.

"Sarah, where are you? Did you talk to Matt?"

I remembered I'd told her I'd call him. "Not yet. I'm upstairs and heading down. Is Mrs. Chan still there?"

"Yes, everyone's here. They've been calling around and comparing notes. The cafe's turned into a command center. Someone saw Tony two hours ago walking along the county road, heading toward town."

"I'll be right down. Tell everyone to stay put. I have good news."

I hung up before Janie could ask more and rose to my feet.

"Okay, Tony, time to set the plan in motion."

Tony carefully shifted Mr. Snuggles from his lap to the sofa, gave him a friendly goodbye pat, and stood up.

I grabbed the metal box and crammed it into

my handbag. It fit, but the bag looked overstuffed and frankly suspicious.

Tony shook his head. "They'll notice."

"I know." Frowning, I took the handbag into the entry foyer, grabbed a red wool scarf from the coat stand, slid the scarf through the handbag handles, and tried to drape it artfully.

Tony shrugged. "That should work."

"It'll have to." I led him back downstairs and paused at the cafe door. "Final check. Ready?"

"Ready."

"Then here we go." I pushed open the door and stepped inside.

Janie saw me first from behind the counter, where she was setting a fresh-baked apple pie in the display case.

Mom glanced over from her spot at the register.

Hialeah looked over from her preferred table near the front window.

Gabby was in her booth with Mrs. Chan and Mr. Benson, arguing heatedly over something as usual.

I cleared my throat. "Everyone, I have news."

Heads turned. Gabby fixed me with a stern glare. "Where have you been?" she barked. "We've been waiting!"

"I have someone with me."

With a dramatic flourish, I stood aside as Tony stepped into the cafe.

Everyone let out a roar of surprise.

"Tony!" Mrs. Chan cried as she struggled out of the booth. "You're alive!"

Tony blinked back tears as he ran to his grandma and gave her a big hug. "I'm fine, Grandma."

"Are you sure?" Mrs. Chan asked, pulling back to look him over. "You're not hurt?"

"I'm fine. Promise."

"You had us so worried."

"I'm sorry."

"You should be sorry!" she snapped, anger surfacing as her fear for his safety receded. "Where have you been?"

I slipped my handbag under the cash register and spoke up. "Tony's been through quite an ordeal, I'm afraid. He came face-to-face with the murderer and spent the night hiding."

Mrs. Chan gasped. "Tony!"

As everyone chimed in with expressions of shock and concern, Mrs. Chan pulled him in for another tight hug. "Oh, my poor boy."

Gabby's eyes were bright with curiosity and calculation. "Such a brave young man," she said solicitously. "What you endured is terrible. Just terrible. You sit yourself down. We're going to get you something to eat. Janie, get this young man a plate of your famous pancakes. Lots of butter, lots of syrup!"

Janie glanced at me and I gave her a quick nod. I knew what Gabby wanted — the full skinny on Tony's eventful evening, pronto — and I also knew she'd let nothing stand in her way.

"Pancakes coming right up," Janie said, then retreated into the kitchen.

"We should call the sheriff," Mr. Benson said cautiously. "He needs to know Tony is here."

"Not yet," Gabby said. "We need to make sure Tony's okay. We can't just toss this poor boy into the vicious clutches of law enforcement. Not after the ordeal he's just been through. Right, Ellie?"

"Right," Mrs. Chan said, clearly as eager as Gabby to learn what had happened. "Food first, then we call the sheriff."

I hid a smile. This was going just as I'd hoped. Tony could practice his edited tale with the gang here in the cafe before being questioned by Matt.

"Does that sound okay to you, Tony?" I said to him.

"Sure." In a matter of seconds he was packed tight in the booth, his grandma at his side, facing an eager Gabby and a curious Mr. Benson.

Mom left the register and pulled up a chair next to the booth, joined a few seconds later by Hialeah, neither of them willing to miss a word.

Tony blinked as he took in his audience. Had he ever faced such avid interest from so many grownups at once? "I don't know where to start," he said nervously.

"Tony came to me," I said, stepping in to smooth his way. "He was worried he might be blamed by the sheriff for what happened at the ice cabin."

"Can't fault the boy for that, can we?" Gabby muttered darkly. "That's how the law rolls. Always rushing to judgment, blaming innocent victims —"

"Gabby," Mr. Benson said.

"Quiet, old man, and stop interrupting. Why are you always so rude?" She swiveled toward me. "Sarah, you were saying?"

I tried to hide a smile — if anyone had a penchant for rudeness, it was a certain octogenarian with a predilection for bright flowered print dresses.

I cleared my throat. "I was saying, Tony remembered his grandma mentioning that I helped catch Jerry's killer. He also heard I know the sheriff pretty well, so he decided to come here and ask for my help."

This was the first of the four lies that Tony and I had chosen to tell. I watched carefully to see how the lie was received.

"Good decision," Gabby said approvingly to Tony. "Sarah's aces when it comes to smacking down killers."

"Gabby," I said, trying to stop her.

"Did she tell you she clocked the maniac who

murdered Jerry? Tackled her and knocked her out cold, right here in the basement?"

Tony's eyes widened — clearly he hadn't heard the details. He glanced at me for confirmation.

"I got lucky," I said quickly. "And I had help."

At that moment, Janie bustled from the kitchen with a heaping plate of pancakes and set them down, along with a bottle of maple syrup and a slab of butter.

"Does this look okay, Tony?" she asked.

"This looks awesome, thank you, ma'am," he said politely.

Mrs. Chan beamed at him, pleased by his manners.

My stomach rumbled as the pancakes' heavenly aroma reached me.

We all watched Tony dig in. I smiled, relieved. Lie Number One had apparently passed muster.

My phone vibrated and I reached into my coat pocket.

My pulse quickened: *Claire.*

"Tony," I said, "why don't you tell them what happened yesterday, starting with when the victim called the restaurant to place a delivery order for dinner?"

He held my gaze for a long second, his mouth full of pancakes.

I got this, his eyes said.

Then, between bites, he launched into his tale.

As quietly as I could, I inched away from the gang and slipped into the building hallway. After closing the door behind me, I answered the phone. "Hey."

"Sarah, what's up?" Wherever Claire was, the connection wasn't good. Static filled the line.

"Have you heard?" I asked.

"Yes, just. You were on the scene?"

"Purely by chance, I swear." What sounded like an engine — a jet engine, perhaps? — blasted through the phone. "Where are you? Is that a plane?"

"You said you got your hands on something?"

"Yes, a box."

"What kind of box?"

"Metal. Locked. About the size and shape of a cigar box."

"Did you open it?"

"No."

"Where are you now?"

"At the cafe."

"Who else knows about the box?"

"The person who gave it to me and that's it."

"Who's that?"

"A teenage kid. He's fine — he's safe — but he's been through a lot."

"How'd he get the box?"

"He was at the crime scene before me — he was

there to make a delivery — and took the box with him."

For a few seconds, Claire was silent and all I could hear was the roar of the engine — if that's what it was — in the background. I pictured her on an airport tarmac, standing next to a private jet, pacing back and forth as she figured out what to say and do next.

"Sarah," she finally said. "Does Matt know about the box?"

"No. We haven't called him yet."

"What will the kid tell him?"

"We just spent an hour practicing his story."

"Practicing?"

"Certain details have been … edited out, shall we say. For example, we're not mentioning the box."

I sensed her doubt over the phone.

"He can do it," I said. "Listen, it's the best I could come up with. If stuff slips, hey, at least we tried. But there's something else."

"Sarah, I have to go. Tell me fast."

"One of the victims — the guy named Howard — wasn't dead when the kid got to the ice cabin. He told the kid something."

"What did he say?" Her tone was sharp, urgent.

"He told the kid to take the box and run. He said the killer couldn't be allowed to get it. He said to bring it to — direct quote — 'Claire's friend at the cafe.'"

There was a long pause as Claire absorbed the full import of those fateful words.

"Also," I said, "just to confirm, you know how the bodies were hooked deliberately?"

"Yes."

"'Hear no evil, see no evil, speak no evil?'"

I heard her sigh, even through the static. "Yes, that seems to be the message."

"Is the message aimed at your organization?"

"Very likely. Did the kid get a good look at the killer?"

"He didn't see his face, but he said he's a big white guy with a dark beard who handles himself well."

"Is the box in your possession?"

"Right here, stuffed in my handbag."

"I'll be there in eighteen hours." The engine-like sound got louder. "But right now, here's what I need you to do."

CHAPTER 11

What Claire needed me to do was — *nothing.* A big fat zippo, nada, zilch. She didn't want me digging deeper. I'd already done too much, she told me. The best thing for me to do now was to sit quietly, hands tucked safely beneath my rear end, and stop nosing around. She'd be in Eagle Cove soon.

I tried pushing back, of course, but she shut me down — predictably — with her usual national security blah blah blah, along with a heaping side dish of personal safety blah blah blah.

And then she hung up.

Alone in the hallway, I could only stare at my phone in disbelief.

Her stance was aggravating — almost insulting. Like she didn't trust me to handle myself. She was sounding like Matt, with a worried dash of Mom tossed in for good measure.

For a long moment, as I paced up and down the hallway, I stewed mightily.

And yet I was finally forced to concede — very grudgingly — that Claire and Matt (and Mom) had a point. I wasn't in law enforcement and I wasn't a spy. Taking on a killer was dangerous. The safest option was to let the experienced professionals handle this.

Still, I argued with myself, playing devil's advocate, what if that wasn't right? What if doing nothing was exactly the *wrong* thing to do? When it came to investigating murder, weren't the first forty-eight hours key? Wasn't it possible that, at this very moment, the killer was disposing of evidence and covering his tracks?

The more I considered that important point, the more apparent it became that my well-intentioned advisers were failing to appreciate the urgency of the situation. They hadn't heard the panic in Tony's voice as he described the terrifying scene in the ice cabin. They hadn't picked up a fishing pole and reeled in a corpse. They didn't have the same visceral connection to the case that I did.

Before hanging up, Claire had told me to expect a call from her colleague Edgar. She was going to arrange for him to swing by the cafe to pick up the metal box, probably that evening.

Unsure how I felt about that, I quietly slipped back into the cafe. The gang was still crowded around the booth, eagerly absorbing Tony's (mostly) true tale.

As I listened in, I was relieved to hear him sticking to the script. We'd agreed that the truth was the best option, with four necessary edits:

First, we weren't sharing the reason Tony came to me. Instead of revealing that the victim begged Tony to take the metal box to "Claire's friend at the cafe," we were leaving Claire and the spy angle out of the story. Instead, he was going to tell everyone that he knew I'd been involved in catching Jerry's killer and heard I got along well with the sheriff, so he thought of me as a good person to ask for help.

Second, we decided not to mention the metal box. With three men dead and a killer on the loose, Tony wanted nothing to do with the box and eagerly went along with my idea to hand it over to Claire.

Third, we weren't going to mention the GPS tracker the killer placed on Tony's truck. If the sheriff and his department found it, so be it. But there was no point in Tony bringing it up, and no point in relaying his suspicions about what the tracker indicated about the killer.

Fourth, we agreed to keep quiet about where Tony spent the night. As much as I disapproved of him and his friends sneaking into empty vacation homes to play video games, I also didn't want him getting into trouble. So in exchange for not tattling, I extracted a firm promise that he and his pals would cut it out. And after a bit of thought, we landed on a plausible alternate overnight shelter: a garage with a busted lock behind the gas station.

In the booth, Tony had reached the part of the story about hiding in the woods. I leaned close to Mom and murmured in her ear, "I think it's time to call Matt."

She sighed with relief. "I'll do that now."

As she scooted into the kitchen for some privacy, the cafe door opened and Mayor Johnson stepped inside.

"Sarah," she said, "I need to speak with your mother."

"I'll get her."

As I was turning to do so, Mom returned from the kitchen. "Betsy's sending over a deputy." Then she saw the mayor. "Doris, is something wrong?"

"Nancy," the mayor said, "I'm sorry, but I need you back at the office. The sheriff and I just spoke. A student's missing and may be —"

Her voice broke off as her gaze landed on the booth — and Tony.

"Tony Chan?" she said, eyes widening.

"Hi, Mayor Johnson," Tony replied.

The mayor stepped closer. "Are you all right?"

"I'm fine, ma'am."

"The sheriff told me you —" Abruptly, she stopped herself. "Why are you here?"

"Because of Sarah," Tony replied immediately, the lie flowing easily. "I figured she could help me out, what with her knowing the sheriff and helping solve that other case."

The mayor blinked, clearly thrown by his answer. "You're saying that, instead of calling the sheriff, instead of calling your parents, you came here to see Sarah?"

Tony blinked, his nervousness returning. "Yeah, that's right."

The mayor stared at him for a long moment, still troubled, then shifted her attention to me. "Sarah," she began, then stopped again, as if trying to puzzle something out. "I don't know why someone would think that you would be…."

And then — *bingo*. It was like a light went on in her head.

She breathed in. "I see it now. You're a…."

I tensed, waiting for her to continue.

"A murder magnet," she exhaled, as if shocked by what she was saying.

"I'm a *what*?"

"It's an actual thing," she said, staring at me like I was a newly discovered species. "A real, documented phenomenon. At a mayor's conference last year, there was an entire session devoted to people like you."

"People like *me*?" I said, starting to get upset.

"Yes. People who...." She paused as she realized that the entire room was listening to her every word.

"People who *what*?" I repeated.

The mayor took a deep breath. "There are people in this world who, often through no fault of their own, attract trouble." She shot an uncomfortable glance at Mom. "I say this not to cast blame. I know you are a good person, Sarah. Decent, hard-working, good-hearted. I am grateful you and Janie reopened Emily's Eats. The entire town is grateful."

"Thank you. But...."

"But certain realities cannot be ignored." She drew herself to her full height. "My job is to protect Eagle Cove's hard-earned reputation as a family-friendly tourist destination."

"How does that relate to me?" I said, even as I saw exactly how it related to me.

"Since returning to Eagle Cove four short months ago, you've been involved in multiple murders."

"Accidentally," I protested.

The mayor was undeterred. Now that she'd figured out her course of action, she was plowing forward in her usual relentless fashion. "When Tony showed up, did you call the sheriff?"

"We called it in," I said, glancing at Mom.

"Right away?"

I swallowed, unwilling to respond.

"Sarah," the mayor said. "What you have done here this morning could be construed as deliberately and actively interfering in a law enforcement investigation."

"Well, I'm not sure that's a fair way to —"

"You very well may be endangering yourself and others by inserting yourself into situations in which you do not belong."

"Hang on," I said, preparing to defend myself even as the truth of her statements sank in.

"Again," the mayor said. "I want to be very clear about this." She glanced again at Mom, whose mouth was set in a thin line that I knew from a lifetime of experience meant she was upset — at me? at the mayor? at both of us? — and trying mightily to keep a lid on it.

"What I am saying, Sarah, is not about blame."

Sure sounds like it is, I didn't say.

I cleared my throat. "Then what are you saying?"

"I'm saying your demonstrated ability and

willingness to involve yourself in dangerous situations is a cause of concern for the citizens of Eagle Cove."

"You're saying I'm a menace," I said as evenly as I could. "A public menace."

"No," the mayor said. "Again, I want to be clear. This is not a matter of blame or intent. I know you mean well. But you worry me, Sarah. Without intending to, you attract trouble."

"You make it sound like I'm cursed or something."

The mayor sighed and shook her head. "I've offended you. I apologize. I should have thought this matter through before speaking. I'll return when I'm better prepared."

The mayor turned to Tony. "I'm very glad you're safe, young man."

"Thank you, ma'am."

"When the sheriff arrives, I expect you to answer his questions fully and completely."

"Yes, ma'am."

The mayor swung her gaze back to me. "We'll talk later. But I'll leave you with a piece of advice."

"Advice?" I repeated.

"You grew up here. I'm surprised I need to remind you."

"Remind me of what?"

"Of a simple but important truth about small towns like ours."

I felt my cheeks flame red — because I knew what she was going to say.

"And that truth is?"

"Some stones," the mayor said solemnly, "are best left unturned."

CHAPTER 12

For a few long seconds after the mayor swept out of the cafe with Mom in tow, silence reigned. Eyes darted to and fro as everyone waited for someone else to speak first.

I knew in my bones what they were all thinking: The mayor wasn't wrong. Small towns have secrets. Sometimes, it was best for those secrets to remain buried.

But the mayor was definitely wrong about *me*. I was no murder magnet, and I definitely wasn't a public menace.

I was about to proclaim as much when Gabby cleared her throat and said, "Maybe you're right, Sarah."

"Right about what?" I said warily.

"Maybe you're cursed."

"Gabby —" Mr. Benson said.

"Oh, be quiet, old man. You know what I mean."

"No, I don't."

"It would explain so much."

"You can't think that —"

"I can't think what?" she said, gearing up for battle. "Since when am I not allowed to *think*? I'm a free thinker, always have been and always will be, and if you ever try to stop me from —"

"Woman, will I ever experience a day in which you do not mangle and twist my words?"

"The day your words start making sense."

Even as Mr. Benson harrumphed his objection, Gabby whirled toward Hialeah. "Let's ask the expert. Our very own ghost-talker."

Every eye in the room swiveled to Hialeah, who stiffened with caution.

"Hialeah, dear," Gabby said, her tone a combination of silk and steel, "we need you to tell us. Is poor Sarah cursed? Are gangs of grumpy ghosts out to get her? Is she haunted by horrors from the great beyond?"

"No," Hialeah said immediately, shooting me a pained glance. "The spirit realm has no issue with Sarah."

"Thank you," I said drily.

Gabby wasn't ready to let her new theory go.

"You sure about that? Aren't ghosts awfully tough to pin down? Maybe we should do a seance."

To my surprise, Hialeah didn't immediately disagree. She gazed at Gabby speculatively. "Perhaps we should. Let me consult."

I tensed as Hialeah closed her eyes and went still. All of us watched, fascinated despite ourselves, as our New Orleans transplant breathed in deeply and then exhaled.

Finally, after a long silence, she opened her eyes. "The spirits tell me Sarah needs to focus on the world of the living."

"That's not helpful," Gabby said. "The world's a big place. We need details!"

Hialeah shook her head. "They'll share more when they're ready."

"Bah," Gabby said. "What good's a direct line to Ghost Town if all they cough up is vague mumbo-jumbo?"

"Listen," I said, jumping in. "Right now we don't need to worry ourselves about the spirit world or the mayor or me or anything else. What we need to do is remember the most important thing of all: Tony is safe and sound."

"Amen," Mrs. Chan murmured, squeezing her grandson's arm.

"We should all be pleased about how we joined forces to find him. Civic-minded engagement, working together for a common cause — what we did here this morning was good work. We should take pride in that."

"An admirable sentiment, ably expressed," Mr. Benson said.

"Darn tootin'," Gabby threw in.

"But," I added, "the mayor is right. Now that Tony is safe, it's time for us to stand aside and let the sheriff and his deputies do their jobs."

Except for one final task, I didn't add.

Mrs. Chan cleared her throat. "I want to thank all of you for your help this morning. Each of you has my everlasting gratitude and appreciation."

"Same here," Tony said, his gaze on me. "Especially Sarah."

"Hear, hear," Mr. Benson said.

I rubbed my hands together. "So that settles it. While we wait for the sheriff's deputy to arrive, I say we get back to our regular routines."

Except for me, I didn't add.

After a short pause to commemorate the moment, the gang let out a collective sigh and allowed normalcy to flow back into the cafe. Janie scooted off to the kitchen, Mr. Benson returned to his seat at the counter, and Hialeah retreated to her table at the front window. Gabby whipped out her phone and began regaling her listener with a loud and boisterous recap of what she'd just learned.

I headed to the cash register, debating what I should do next about the mysterious metal box in my handbag, hidden only by the red scarf draped over it.

The idea to leave the box here and wait for Claire's colleague Edgar to collect it didn't seem right. In fact, as plans go, it seemed almost dangerous. The killer had gone to a lot of trouble to get his hands on the box. With his dying breath, Howard had begged Tony to take it to Claire. I had no idea who the killer was, but I knew he was ruthless and — I flashed to the hook deliberately imbedded in Howard's lip — twisted.

I blinked with surprise as I realized what I intended to do.

Before I could ponder further, Hialeah rose from her seat at the front table and approached the cash register.

"Sarah," she said softly.

"Yes, Hialeah?"

She glanced at the others to make sure they weren't paying attention, then continued in a low voice. "What I said is true. The spirits are not the source of your troubles."

"That's good to hear."

She waited silently for me to catch up.

It took me a few seconds. "But the spirits are saying I have troubles. And they know the source."

"They shared a vision," she said, her voice barely a whisper.

"A vision?"

"Of you and your soulmate."

My heart started racing. "My soulmate?"

She nodded solemnly. "Not everyone is blessed with a second chance. The two of you have found each other again. If you open yourselves to the promise of the present, you may find the happiness that eluded you before."

"Okay," I said, trying to ignore the welling of hope rushing up within me. If she was talking about Matt, and if what she was saying had even a grain of truth….

Her gaze froze on the red scarf draped over my handbag. "That color. I saw it in my vision. Along with a deeper red." Her eyes flashed with worry. "Blood red."

"I don't see how…."

"I saw the two of you in grave danger. I sensed the energy of a troubled soul, desperate and angry, lashing out."

A tingle of dread crept up my spine. "Hialeah…."

"A soul unmasked and bare. Desperate to remain hidden, but with anger impossible to ignore."

She reached out and gripped my hand. "You must be careful. Both of you."

"Careful?" I said, my chest tightening.

"I felt pain and fear, exploding on an empty plain. A struggle, a tangle of red." She squeezed my hand, her eyes filled with worry. "I'm sorry. That's all I saw. The vision wasn't clear."

"But you're saying...."

"What I'm saying, Sarah, is please, be very careful."

CHAPTER 13

It wasn't every day that a psychic warned me of imminent danger. In fact, Hialeah's urgent plea counted as my first-ever spirit-inspired alert.

I didn't actually believe what she was telling me, of course — seeing into the future isn't possible, right? — but my New Orleans friend's anxiety definitely felt real. Touched by her concern, I thanked her and then slipped into the kitchen to ask Janie if she could hold down the fort while I went to talk with Matt to smooth the way for Tony. When Janie agreed, I grabbed my handbag, rushed upstairs for my winter coat and gloves, then headed back down and dashed across the street to my car, managing to hop in seconds before Deputy Martinez pulled up in front of the cafe.

After watching the deputy hurry inside, I reached into the glove compartment for my map book. It took a few seconds to find what I was looking for: the Middlemore University campus.

The map showed three college buildings bordering the state park. Assuming Tony and his high-school pals were right, one of those buildings was a top-secret government facility. To identify which one, I'd have to check them out in person.

I looked up from the map, torn by indecision. *Was this really what I wanted to do?*

Through the cafe window, I watched the gang circling Deputy Martinez like a pack of wolves preparing to pounce. From the mixture of consternation and resignation on the deputy's face, I knew she was being peppered with unfair and accusatory questions, Gabby leading the charge.

My attention was drawn to a figure bustling down Main Street toward the cafe. It was Mrs. Bunch, a charter member of Gabby's octogenarian gaggle.

I let out a sigh. Mrs. Bunch would be only the first of many arrivals. Once Eagle Cove's gossip brigade got hold of the news, Emily's Eats would become an irresistible lure for those seeking all the juicy details.

That settled it. Claire's plan wasn't going to work. Having her colleague Edgar come to the cafe for the metal box wasn't a good idea.

It was definitely time for Plan B. I pulled out my phone, dialed Claire, and got voicemail. "The cafe's crazy-crowded and not the place for me to meet your friend. Gossipers are descending as we speak. Instead of your friend coming to me, I'll bring what I have to him. Call when you get this."

Decision made, I started the car and pulled out. At the next corner, I turned off Main Street — Matt would likely be heading to the cafe soon, and I didn't want him to see me driving away — and took residential streets to the main county road.

After looking both ways and finding the coast clear, I turned north toward Middlemore.

In the months since returning to Eagle Cove, I'd become very familiar with this thirty-minute drive. A college town with a fun vibe, Middlemore is twice the size of Eagle Cove and also where my sister Grace lives with her husband and three kids. Over the holidays, Mom and I had driven there for a number of family and Christmas events. In the past month, with the cafe consuming my every waking moment, I'd managed to make it over only once, for the twelfth birthday dinner for Grace's eldest, Danny.

With a start, I realized I hadn't called Grace yet to tell her about my eventful evening and morning. Talk about a crazy eighteen hours!

As I hit the twisty switchbacks rising up and over Heartsprings Ridge, I weighed giving her a call. Maybe I could even swing by her office — she worked as an administrator at the university — for a quick coffee.

No, I decided after a moment's consideration. Now wasn't the right time. Until the box was safely in Edgar's hands, it was best to keep everyone, including my sister, out of this.

Unless — the thought came like a flash — *she could help me.*

It was only as I was reaching for the car's dashboard to dial her that I realized my hand was trembling.

I blinked with surprise — why was my hand shaking? — then gasped as a wave of emotion surged through me, unexpected and powerful.

As much as I hated admitting it, I knew what was going on. Through hard-won experience, I'd learned there was only so much pretense and denial I was capable of carrying at any given time. Very clearly, I'd reached my limit.

Sarah, Sarah, Sarah, I chastised myself. *When will you ever stop fooling yourself into believing you're strong?*

My eyes teared up. Despite working overtime to keep my head clear and my feelings in check, the events of the past eighteen hours had managed to slip through my defenses. The murders on the lake had upset me. Tony's brush with violent death had frightened me. Hialeah's warning had unsettled me. The mayor's accusation had bothered me.

And the fish hook imbedded in Howard's lip

— that troubled me in a way I was only beginning to understand. Would I ever be able to banish that horrible image from my mind? What in the world did the hooked lip even mean? Clearly, the killer was sending a message. But to whom? And why?

It was only as the switchbacks ended and I crested the ridge that I felt my tension ease. The road straightened. My breathing gradually returned to normal and my heart rate with it.

At some point, I told myself, *you need to own up to your many flaws. You'll be a lot better off when you do.*

If there was a silver lining in this situation, it was that my involvement in this deadly affair was nearing an end. As soon as I handed over the metal box to Edgar, I was done.

The thought was comforting. Plus, I heard myself proposing, maybe the small role I'd played in this mess could even be deemed … beneficial? Was it reasonable for me to feel okay about what I'd done to deliver Tony to safety and keep Claire's spy organization out of the picture?

Maybe, I allowed.

I waited to see if that fragile proposition survived the next few seconds. When it did, I hurriedly used the car dashboard to call Grace.

She picked up on the first ring. "Hey, you."

"Hey," I said, striving for a normal tone. "Got a minute?"

"I have a meeting in four, but what's up?"

A smile crept to my lips. Precision is one of Grace's many superpowers, part of the arsenal she deploys to skillfully manage a demanding job, three rambunctious kids, and an absent-minded professor husband. One might think that I, as the older sister, would be the more responsible sibling. But no — my younger sister is our family's true organizing genius.

So when she said she had four minutes, that's how many minutes she had.

I cleared my throat. "I'm wondering if you've heard about the three men who died on the lake last night."

"A bit, yes." There was a pause. "Don't tell me you're involved."

"Afraid so." As quickly as I could, I relayed the key points.

"Oh, gosh, Sarah," she said when I finished. "I'm so sorry you had to go through that. How are you holding up?"

"I'm fine," I lied. "All good."

"I assume Mom is…?"

"Worried sick, of course. As usual."

Her sigh came through loud and clear. "I'll give you both a call tonight."

"Before you go, quick question. Which building did the three men work in? The cafe is sending a box of muffins to their colleagues as an expression of sympathy."

"They worked in the Applied Sciences laboratory. You need the address?"

"No, I can get it. Thanks."

"No prob." There was a pause. "Um, Sarah?"

"Yes?"

"Please tell me the muffins are the only reason you want the address."

"Totally," I lied.

"Sarah," she said, her voice rising. "This is one thing Mom's right about. You really need to stop trying to —"

"Oops," I said, cutting her off. "Another call. Talk to you tonight. Love you. Bye!"

"Sarah, don't —"

"Bye!"

I clicked off and stared guiltily at the car dashboard. Grace sensed I was up to something, obviously. Just like everyone else always seemed to.

Was I really that transparent and predictable?

The answer, just as obviously, was a resounding *yes*.

Irritated, I shook my head. I was going to have to do something about my reputation for nosiness. After wrapping up this current mess, of course.

For the next few minutes, while the road took me past scenic vistas of snow-dusted forest and farmland, I attempted to turn my attention away from my innumerable failings and toward the task ahead. If Tony's high-school pals were right about the Applied Sciences building being a secret government facility, then it was unlikely I'd get past the lobby. I'd probably need to use the building directory to dial Edgar from the lobby and have him come down. Or, if there was a reception desk, I'd ask for Edgar there.

At the thought of Tony, I felt a tug of unease. Something he'd said earlier hadn't been completely clear. I'd meant to ask him about it but hadn't.

And now I couldn't recall what that something was. *Grrr.*

With downtown Middlemore approaching, I turned my focus to the road. The closer I got to campus, the heavier the traffic. At a red light, I quickly consulted my map, then headed past the university's main buildings onto a quiet road bordering the state park. A few moments later, I caught a glimpse of a large, dark building through the trees and a sign along the road that read, "Graveston Center for Applied Sciences."

With a flutter of anticipation, I turned and headed in.

CHAPTER 14

The entry drive took me through a stand of pine into a large, paved parking area next to a modern, five-story building. The building was smooth and solid in appearance, clad in dark mirrored glass. Despite the early afternoon brightness, the building seemed to absorb the sunlight hitting it.

After a swing through the lot to get my bearings, I parked in a spot away from the lobby entrance. With growing tension, I shut off the engine and contemplated my target. The parking lot was only about a third full. I didn't see anyone outside — no surprise given the frigid temperatures. The building itself seemed rather severe. There was nothing welcoming about its dark mirrored facade. It looked bland and corporate, chilly and uninviting.

I flashed back three months to my surprise visit with Aunt Emily. Claire had driven me to a secret destination and forced me to wear a blindfold, so I had no way of knowing for sure where she'd taken me. But my gut was screaming that she'd brought me here.

Solving that mystery was for another day. My goal right now was simple: Give the metal box to Edgar. I retrieved my phone from my handbag to see if Claire had returned my call — nope, not yet — and was about to slip it back in when it rang, startling me.

With a jolt, I saw it was Matt. Did I dare pick up?

And then I realized —

Did I dare *not*?

Steeling myself, I brought the phone to my ear.

"Hey, Matt," I said as innocently as I could.

"Sarah." In just two syllables, I knew he was angry and trying hard to maintain his patience. "Where are you?"

"Running an errand. Are you calling about Tony?"

"I'm at the cafe. I expected you to be here."

"I'll be heading back soon."

"Not soon, Sarah." His frustration slipped through. "We need you back here *now*."

"Okay," I said brightly. "On my way."

Before he could ask me more, I hung up.

Oh, boy. I closed my eyes and stifled a groan. No doubt about it, I was in deep doo-doo. Barely three hours earlier, I'd promised him — vouchsafed, averred, solemnly sworn — that I was staying out of this murderous mess. Yet here I was, up to my eyeballs and about to dive deeper.

If he ever found out how immersed I truly was....

But he wouldn't, I reassured myself. Not if I completed my task quickly.

Energized, I grabbed my handbag and hopped out of the car, eager to deliver the box to Claire's colleague and be done with this deadly business once and for all. I hurried across the frigid parking lot, handbag over my shoulder. With a quick glance to confirm that the red scarf still obscured the shape of the metal box within, I pulled open the lobby's glass door and stepped inside.

It was only then that I realized my mistake.

At the far end of the lobby, near the elevator bank, stood a long desk staffed by three men — security guards, I presumed — dressed in identical blue blazers. The men looked tough and capable, the kind of guys who could squash me like a bug with their pinkie fingers. One of the men was Black and the other two were — the thought hit me like a sledgehammer — bearded white guys who matched Tony's description of the killer.

You shouldn't have come here, I told myself. Followed immediately by —

Don't leap to conclusions.

My heart started pounding. Shakily, I started across the lobby. Half the men in New England matched Tony's description of the killer, I tried to tell myself. The "burly lumberjack" look was very much in vogue these days. Odds were low that, with each step across the lobby, I was approaching the killer.

Still, I couldn't ignore the feeling of danger. The victims had most likely known their murderer. It was quite possible they'd worked with him.

Wouldn't it be safest for me to assume that one of the two bearded white guys behind the desk was the culprit?

My mental ping-pong match ended as I reached the security desk. The guards eyed me curiously.

I gave them a smile, hoping I was coming across as normal and not quietly freaked out.

"Hi," I said in a cheerful tone. "I'm here to see —"

In the split second before the next word left my mouth, I realized I was about to make an even bigger mistake.

"Yes, ma'am?" one of the bearded guards said, prompting me.

Should I?

No.

But then my only remaining option is to say —

"Claire," I said. "I'm here to see Claire Emerson."

The three men went still, just for a fraction of a second. The same guard said, "I'm not familiar with that name."

"I'm a friend of hers from school," I said, the words spilling out of me like water from a babbling brook. "Elementary school, actually. We were best friends for like forever, but then she moved away. We both grew up here. Well, not here, but over in Eagle Cove."

The guard's quizzical expression didn't change.

I continued as breezily as I could. "I bet you know her. Tall, blond, beautiful, stylish? She did some work here recently — last fall — but I heard this morning from a friend that she's back and I figured hey, why not swing by?"

"You said she works here?" the guard asked.

"I'm not sure, but I think this is the place?" I said, trying to sound unsure. "She told me she's coming up for a visit and I thought she was getting here tomorrow, but then I heard from Mavis that she might already be here and since I was heading over anyway to see my sister — my sister works at the university, she's an administrator — I thought, why not give it a try?"

"Give it a try?"

"You know, try to see her."

The Black guard spoke up. "We can ask around for you." His voice was warm and low. With a friendly smile, he gestured to a low bench near the lobby windows. "Why don't you take a seat? Shouldn't take long."

"Sure," I said brightly.

I made my way to the bench and settled in, hoping against hope that I was coming across as calm and carefree and innocent of all subterfuge. The urge to adjust the draping of the red scarf over my handbag was nearly irresistible, but I managed to focus instead on my nails, which I realized actually required some attention.

After conferring quietly, the two bearded guards slipped away and the Black guard spoke up. "Ma'am, can I ask for your name?"

"Sarah Boone."

He gave me another friendly smile. "We get a fair number of visitors. If your friend is one of them, we'll see if we can track her down for you."

"Thank you."

He got up from the desk and crossed the lobby to join me at the bench. From his stride, I saw that my initial impression of him — thirties, tall, fit — was spot-on.

"I've been to Eagle Cove a couple of times," he said as he sat down. "Great little town." He had a nice face, open and engaging. His manner was relaxed. He was trying to come across as a regular guy with a boring job who was eager to pass the time with casual chit-chat.

But I knew what he was really up to, or at least I was pretty sure.

Still, since he'd picked the conversational topic, I went with it.

"I take it you're new to the area?"

"Moved here last year."

"Oh, where from?"

"Atlanta."

"How's New England treating you?"

"So far, so good. I'm looking forward to getting to know the area better, including Eagle Cove."

"Lots to do in our little town," I said, playing along. "It's a bit quieter than Middlemore, at least this time of year."

In the conversation that followed, his manner remained relaxed and his tone friendly. His questions about Eagle Cove were exactly what one would expect from someone who'd recently moved here.

For my part, I could only hope I was successfully coming across as Claire's agenda-free childhood friend, chatty and clueless and maybe a bit scattered.

We heard a buzz from the desk and the guard dashed over. He picked up a phone and listened, then turned to me. "Sounds like your friend Claire was part of a consulting team that did some work for the university a few months back."

"Yes, that's right," I said eagerly, rising to my feet and joining him at the security desk. "She's a consultant. She told me she was doing a big data project — or something like that? — for the university."

"That makes sense. She was actually working out of a different building, not this one. The engineering building, they told me."

"Oh," I said, trying to sound disappointed. "Looks like I've bothered you for nothing."

"The person I talked to said she's not actually at the university right now but will be tomorrow, like you originally thought."

"Oh." I gave him a perplexed look. "Then I guess Mavis got it wrong. I guess I should just … call Claire when she gets here?"

"Sounds like."

"Sorry I took up your time. You must think I'm a scatterbrained idiot."

"Of course not. Happy to help."

"Next time you're in Eagle Cove, please stop by the cafe."

He gave me a big grin. "I'll definitely do that."

"Thanks for your help. Hope you have a great afternoon."

"You, too, ma'am."

We gave each other friendly smiles. So much politeness!

Then, as casually as I could, I walked across the lobby and out of the building. With a deliberately normal pace, I headed back to my car.

Heart pounding, I started the engine and drove away.

CHAPTER 15

I nearly cried with relief as the Applied Sciences building receded in my rear-view mirror. I'd made it out!

Then my inner critic, the voice that likes to be my ever-vigilant arbiter of rationality and objectivity, piped up.

Surely you realize you're overreacting, my inner critic drawled snootily. *What actually just happened is that you leaped to a ludicrous conclusion, told a lie, had a banal chat, and left. Surely you appreciate how silly you're being? Surely you understand how pointless your little jaunt was?*

I wasn't being silly, I argued back, rather weakly.

The conversation with the security guard was ridiculous.

I shook my head. *He was testing me.*

My inner critic laughed. *He was just being friendly!*

He had an agenda, I persevered.

After more mocking laughter, I tried turning down the dial on my self-appointed self-criticizer. But no, it wasn't finished.

Let's say you're right about that building being a nest of spies. If it is, you must admit you screwed up by going there.

Agreed, I admitted. The instant I'd seen the two bearded guards, I'd realized my mistake. Hopefully I'd avoided further damage by asking for Claire instead of Edgar. If I was lucky, I'd managed to come across like a clueless, innocent idiot.

Clueless idiot, yes, my inner critic repeated. *On that we agree.*

I reached the county road that would take me back to Eagle Cove and realized something else.

Excitement jolted through me. My inner critic faded away as a different part of my brain — the part that loved playing with crazy ideas — asked: *What if?*

Was it possible that my mistake could, just possibly, be one of those moments in which disaster leads to opportunity?

With rising excitement, I allowed my plan — because that's what it quickly became — to unfold as I headed up and over the ridge. If what I thought had just happened had indeed just happened, then my little plan could work. When the killer showed up, he'd have nowhere to hide.

Just outside Eagle Cove, I realized I was running

low on gas. When I stopped to fill up, I could check to confirm my suspicions.

And if I'm right about it being there, then —

My thoughts were interrupted by a flash of lights in the rear-view mirror, followed by the sharp blare of a siren. A glance back sent my heart racing.

A sheriff's vehicle was zooming up behind me, headlights flashing.

I was being pulled over!

Shocked, I tapped the brakes — had I been speeding? — and hit the turn signal. A stretch of open shoulder appeared ahead.

Heart pounding, I pulled over.

When the truck stopped behind me, I saw who it was and gasped.

Matt!

He jumped out of the truck and headed to my passenger door, his body taut with tension.

Oh, geez. Hurriedly, before he could see me do so, I grabbed my handbag and tossed it in the back seat.

He rapped on the window. "Open up, Sarah."

With a gulp, I unlocked the door.

He slid in next to me, his powerful presence overwhelming the space, then fixed me with an expression full of the emotions he was normally so good at keeping in check — anger, worry, frustration, you name it.

"Hey," I said weakly, trying to meet his gaze. "What's up?"

His nostrils flared with anger. "Where have you been, Sarah?"

"I was in Middlemore."

"What were you doing there?"

I opened my mouth but then shut it when I realized my plan wasn't going to work without adjustment. No way was Matt going to let me out of his sight again. Not after I'd vanished so mysteriously from the cafe.

I'd have to bring him in sooner. Which meant I needed to say —

"I took something last night," I blurted, the words flying from my mouth before I could second-guess myself.

He blinked, thrown by the sudden shift. "You did *what*?"

"I removed something from the crime scene."

His eyes widened. "What did you remove?"

"I can't tell you."

"Why?"

I made my voice sound meek and tiny. "I can't tell you why."

"Sarah." He took a deep breath, visibly willing himself to remain calm, then said angrily, "You haven't been telling me what or why for months."

I froze, taken aback. "What do you mean, for months?"

His furious eyes drilled into me. "No more games."

I felt a rush of panic. "You're talking about...."

"What neither of us is supposed to be aware of."

That's when I realized: *He knew. He'd known all along.* I nearly gasped, though the revelation shouldn't have surprised me. After all, he had eyes and ears and a brain — all of them excellent — and knew how to use them. That head of his was good for a whole lot more than just looking ruggedly handsome.

"Pretty *and* smart," I murmured, hoping desperately to move the conversation to lighter ground. "Go figure."

He was in no mood to be amused. "Sarah...." He stopped, struggling for words, then continued. "What's going on here, beneath the surface of our quiet little town, is no joke."

"I know that."

He shook his head. "I don't think you do. If you knew that — *truly* knew that — then we wouldn't be having this argument."

Heat rose to my cheeks. "Don't think for a second I'm not aware of the stakes."

He didn't budge. "Claire has training and experience."

So he knew about Claire. "Unlike me?"

"Very much unlike you."

I opened my mouth to protest but no words came out. Because what could I say? He was totally, unassailably *right*. I was a rank amateur — zero skills, no background, and completely in the dark.

"Three months ago," he said, "you nearly got killed."

"I survived."

"You got *lucky*."

I flushed. The bald truth of those three little words *hurt*.

He shifted toward me and I found myself wondering if he was going to pull me in for a big hug or slap cuffs on me and arrest me.

But he did neither. Instead he placed a strong hand on my shoulder and leaned closer. In his eyes, I saw anger and worry, but also a vulnerability that took my breath away. "That afternoon last fall," he said, his voice thick with emotion, "when I found you unconscious on the basement floor…."

"Matt…."

"I thought you were dead."

"I'm sorry."

"Sorry doesn't cut it." He swallowed, his eyes brimming with emotion.

He was close enough for me to catch his fresh, clean scent. He'd showered after meeting me at the ice cabin this morning. Shaved, too, judging by the lack of stubble on his strong jaw. In those incredible grey eyes of his, I saw a rush of emotions he was barely able to control.

I almost did it then — I almost kissed him. *Oh my oh my oh my,* I wanted to. In that moment, I wanted nothing more than to wrap my arms around him and press my lips to his and breathe in the heady, masculine, wonderful smell of him.

Don't do it, I implored myself. *Not now. Not yet.*

Swallowing hard, I whispered, "I meant what I said this morning."

"This morning?" he repeated.

"What I told you at the lake."

He blinked, and the swell of emotion receded. His hand left my shoulder. "You mean, when you promised you'd stay out of this one? Swore up and down that these murders were none of your concern?"

"I only got involved because Tony came to me."

"Tony," he said with a sigh, then slid back into his seat, the sheriff in him returning to the fore. "The young Mr. Chan's story has some soft spots."

I tried to look confused. "What do you mean?"

"Sarah...." His tone was weary.

"Sarah what?"

"Stop."

"Stop what?"

"What you're doing."

"You mean ... dancing around the hidden truth?"

His expression said it all: *Yes.*

"Okay," I said. "Let's say, hypothetically, I didn't take anything from the crime scene last night."

He nodded, encouraging me to continue. "And?"

"Let's say, hypothetically, someone else did and handed it over to me."

"And?"

"Let's say, hypothetically, the killer wants this something."

"Okay," he said, grudgingly playing along. "Hypothetically, what is this something?"

I tried not to glance at the back seat. "It's a hypothetical metal box, about the size of a cigar box, solidly built, with a big lock."

He frowned. "Were you able to open it?"

I shook my head. "Hypothetically, I was planning to give it back to its rightful owner. I drove there this afternoon to do so."

Another sigh. "There?"

"Hypothetically, a top-secret location that's really not top-secret if you're a high school student in this town, because apparently they know *everything*."

For a split second, he nearly grinned. "Where?"

"On the edge of the campus, near the state park."

"Where the three victims worked. So you went there and...."

"I was about to hand over the box — I even went inside the building to hand it over — when I realized the rightful owner might be compromised."

He shook his head. "You can't possibly know that."

"You're right," I said immediately. "But hear me out."

"Sarah, you shouldn't be telling me any of this," he growled. "I should be arresting you for what you've done."

"I know. But please, hear me out."

"Where is the metal box now?"

"Somewhere safe," I said, trying to keep my face immobile.

"It's here in the car, isn't it?"

"I never said that."

"Show it to me."

"I'd prefer not to, thank you."

He shifted around as if preparing to check out the back seat, then stopped himself. "How did Tony know he should come to you?"

"You mean, you didn't buy his story about seeking me out due to my reputation as a killer-catcher and sheriff-whisperer?"

"The real reason, please."

I hoped I was right to be sharing this with him. "Hypothetically, one of the victims wasn't dead yet and told Tony to bring the box to me."

He tensed. "The victim told Tony to bring it to *you*?"

"Hypothetically, his exact words were, 'Bring it to Claire's friend at the cafe.'"

I watched as he connected the dots and reached the same conclusion I had.

He sighed heavily. "So you concocted an edited version of events to keep Claire and her colleagues out of it."

"Hypothetically."

"And coached young Mr. Chan."

"Hypothetically."

He sighed again, but this time not in anger. Now he seemed almost regretful. "We shouldn't be doing this."

"Doing what?"

"Any of this. Twisting ourselves into knots to support the hidden efforts of a covert organization we know nothing about."

"I'm doing this for Claire."

He didn't reply. For a long moment we gazed at each other, both of us spent from our confrontation.

He let out a long sigh. "I'm pretty sure you're also doing it for you."

"For me?" I said, resisting the instinctive urge to argue.

"The itch you can't help but scratch. You've never been able to stay away from a mystery."

"Are you going to arrest me?"

"Maybe," he said, his eyes not leaving mine.

"Before you decide," I replied, "hear me out. I have an idea how to flush out the killer."

"Sarah…."

"But first, a question. Did you find the tracker?"

He went still. "On Tony's truck? Yes."

"When I walked into the top-secret building today, there were three guards in the lobby."

"And?"

"For several long minutes, one of them kept me there, asking me lots of questions."

His eyes narrowed. "While the other two…."

"Were checking me out, no doubt. Probably one of them ran a background check and the other went outside to…."

"To take a look at your car."

"If the covert agency is compromised — which I'm guessing it is, based on what the victim said to Tony about Claire — then it's quite possible the three victims were killed by a colleague."

"And?"

"Two of the guards matched Tony's description of the killer. If one of them did it, then he might have…."

Matt sighed. "Put a tracker on your car. Have you looked?"

"Not yet. But we should. It would be awfully nice to find one."

His eyebrows rose. "Nice?"

"My idea to catch the killer depends on it."

He groaned and closed his eyes, steeling himself. "What's your idea?"

I took a deep breath, then dove in. "It's going to require a bit of deception."

CHAPTER 16

We argued, of course. He hated what I proposed, plain and simple, and didn't sugarcoat what worried him.

"Maybe I'm wrong," I said calmly after hearing him out. "Maybe there isn't a tracker on my car."

With a growl, he clambered out and began a careful inspection. When he bent to examine the front right wheel, I saw his shoulders tense. The angry line of his mouth when he rose told me all I needed to know.

We argued more after he got back in. But I knew I was right and held my ground. Yes, there were risks, but they were manageable. We had an advantage over the killer right now. It would be foolish not to make the most of it.

And if the plan didn't work out — if the killer didn't bite — then what was lost?

Gradually, I wore him down. It took a fair amount of persuasion to ease him past the unavoidable fact that the plan would need to involve *me* — i.e., Sarah the meddling murder magnet. But once he got over that hump, he reluctantly agreed the plan had merit and grudgingly hopped on board.

He extracted concessions, of course. He forced me to swear I'd remove myself from the situation as soon I completed the three tasks we agreed I needed to do. He warned me he was going to order his deputies to arrest me if they saw me doing anything — literally anything — other than those three specific tasks.

And he definitely went too far when he informed me I'd be spending the evening with Mom so she could keep tabs on me. "I'm going to have her call me if you leave her sight for even one second," he announced, very firmly.

"Totally unnecessary," I shot back.

"Too bad."

"I feel very untrusted."

He let out a short laugh. "Tough."

Grrrr.

Still, I was pleased with the outcome of our negotiation. Sitting there with him in the car, hashing out what would happen and when, was actually fun. Being with him made me feel energized, engaged, *needed.*

And my feeling this way was largely because of *him*. I was lucky to have this man back in my life. Not only did he accept my many flaws, he was willing to look past them. He had respect for me and faith in me, and for that I was extremely grateful.

Eventually, we ran out of reasons to keep talking. The afternoon light was fading. A lot had to be done to make sure everything was ready for what might be a long night.

Reluctantly, he pushed open the car door and got out. Then he leaned down, his concerned gaze taking me in. "I really should have Deputy Martinez take your place."

"We've been over this. She has a lot of other things to do. I'll be done and away before you know it."

He sighed. "Text me as soon as you —"

"Promise. The very second."

With a final sigh, he shut the car door and walked back to his truck.

And I, with nervous anticipation, started up and headed home, my mind racing over the plan we'd just agreed on.

CHAPTER 17

In theory, the plan was pretty simple. My part involved three tasks.

Task One: Substitute the metal box (currently stuffed in my handbag) with something similar.

When I hit Main Street, I found a parking spot near the cafe and was about to hop out when I realized with a guilty jolt that I'd forgotten to update Janie. I'd been gone for three hours — what must she be thinking?

A text would be better than a call. "So sorry," I typed. "Still working through things with Matt. Big favor to ask: Can you close up today?"

Thankfully, I got her reply right away. "No prob. Hope all's going well. See you tomorrow!"

Relieved, I grabbed my handbag (and the metal box still in it) and dashed to the building. A short glance up and down the street confirmed I hadn't been noticed. As quietly as I could, I opened the hallway door — the last thing I wanted was for Janie or Gabby or Mr. Benson hearing me — then slipped in and headed down to the basement.

The steps creaked ominously as I descended. I suppressed a shudder as stale, musty air assailed me. I wasn't a fan of this space — its association with corpses and killers didn't exactly foster the warm fuzzies — but what I needed was down here and right now that was all that mattered.

I made a beeline for an old wooden shelf along the far wall and found what I'd remembered being there: a small toolbox. I reached into my handbag, took out the metal box, and set it on the shelf next to the old toolbox for a visual comparison. Yes, this would work. Though the boxes weren't exactly the same size, the proportions and coloring were similar and both were made of metal.

Briefly, I considered where to hide Tony's metal box. I could be clever about this or — *nah*, best not to overthink it. Before I could change my mind, I set the metal box on the same shelf and arranged a can of furniture stain in front of it to make it less visible.

Good enough. Then I crammed the replacement toolbox into my handbag and made my way back upstairs.

Time for Task Two. I almost whipped out my phone right there in the hallway but stopped when I realized my voice might carry, so I hurried outside to my car. The sky above was darkening. Night was almost here. Quickly, I availed myself of the wonders of the Internet and found the number for the front desk of the Graveston Center for Applied Sciences.

After taking a deep breath to steady my nerves, I dialed.

"Graveston Center," a man answered after the first ring. His voice, low and steady, sounded like that of the guard I'd spoken with. "How can I help you?"

"Hi, it's Sarah Boone again. Do you remember me? I was there earlier today."

"Of course, ma'am. How can I help you?"

"Can you get a message to Claire Emerson?"

"I can certainly try."

"The real reason I came by your building was to give Claire something. But when I found out she wasn't there I changed my mind. Instead, I'm taking it back to where it came from."

"You're taking *it* back to where it came from?"

"Yes. She'll know."

"Ms. Boone, can I ask why?"

"Because I'm freaking out, that's why," I snapped, my voice rising. "I didn't want to have it and maybe I shouldn't have agreed to take it, but I did and now I don't want this thing anywhere near me."

"Ma'am, I —"

"You don't understand," I continued, practically yelling into the phone. "I left her a voicemail and asked her to call me, but she didn't pick up. She never does. I'm tired of this. I don't want to be involved. Can you let her know?"

"Yes, ma'am, but I —"

"She knows where to get it. Thank you."

Then I hung up.

Heart racing, I reviewed my performance. I'd gotten quite emotional! At least to my ears, I'd sounded convincing.

Feeling relieved and pleased, I texted Matt. "Call made. Heading there now."

If the call to the Applied Sciences building was recorded — and I expected it was — then it was likely that Claire's secret spy organization would want to learn more. They'd ask the three security guards about my visit this afternoon. They'd call Claire (if they'd hadn't already) to see what she knew. They'd want to find out what "it" was and where I was taking it.

With inquiries going out, it was possible the killer would be among those who learned about my frantic call.

I was hoping for that, in fact.

Because my frantic call would line up with the information that would soon be transmitted by the tracker placed on my car.

Which brought me to Task Three. I was about to pull out when my phone buzzed. I frowned when I saw it was Mom — now was not a good time — but picked up anyway.

"Hey," I said.

"Sarah, I just got off the phone with Matt and he told me I have to keep an eye on you tonight."

Grrr.

"Yes, that's right," I said, choosing to honor the terms of the agreement. "Are you okay with that?"

"Of course!" Her voice sounded chipper, even excited. "We can have lasagna."

My stomach growled and I realized I was starving. Mom's lasagna was hearty and delicious — I couldn't think of a better meal for a frigid February evening.

"I'd love that. See you in an hour?"

"Perfect. Love you, dear."

"Love you, too."

Then I set the phone on the car seat, started the engine, and began my third and final task.

CHAPTER 18

Task Three was simple, at least on the surface. All I had to do was drive my car to the lake and leave the metal box (the replacement box, that is) in the ice cabin. And then drive away.

The tracker on the car would trace my movements. If the killer had access to the tracking information — and chances were pretty decent that he did — then he would know I returned to the lake. If he also found out about my frantic call, then he'd put the pieces together and act. He'd already murdered three times for the metal box, so clearly he was willing to go to extreme lengths to get his hands on it.

If he did come back, he'd be stepping into a trap. Exposed and alone on the open ice, he'd have nowhere to run when Matt and his deputies emerged from their hiding spots along the wooded shore and surrounded him.

And with the killer apprehended and in custody, this frightening, tumultuous day would draw to a close.

There were a lot of assumptions baked into this plan, of course. Much of it — especially what the killer would learn about my movements and motives — was pure guesswork.

But there was a fair chance it would play out as we hoped. If the killer was as desperate and determined as he seemed, he'd get his hands on the clues and feel compelled to follow them.

And if he didn't?

Then Matt and his team would spend a long, dark, fruitless night outside in the freezing cold, waiting for a killer who didn't show up.

I certainly was hoping for the former as I approached the marina. The night was dark and the gravel lot empty of vehicles.

I parked in front of the shack. Despite the comfy warmth of my car, I found myself shivering. Matt had told me to expect to see nothing when I arrived. Setting a trap for a dangerous killer was no simple matter. He and his deputies had a lot to do to get ready. When I arrived, he told me, he'd be in hiding somewhere nearby, watching and waiting.

Anxiously, I grabbed my phone and texted him as promised. "I'm here. How about you?"

I looked around anxiously. Was he in the surrounding woods, perhaps setting up a perimeter? I paused, struck by the thought. Which cop show or military movie had taught me those words? Did I have even the faintest idea what "setting up a perimeter" meant?

For a long moment, my overactive brain wasted time on that and other pointless musings as I waited for Matt to emerge from his hiding spot — or at least text me — and set me at ease.

But my phone stayed silent and no Matt appeared.

Out on the lake, the ice cabin was barely visible. Heavy clouds covered the moon. The forecast was predicting a light snow.

It was hard to believe that twenty-four hours earlier, I'd been parked in this very spot, getting ready to set out across the ice to deliver a box of freshly baked muffins to a group of ice fishermen.

For a split second, I caught a flash of light in the ice cabin window — like someone had adjusted the curtain. Maybe Matt was there for a final check, making sure all was ready? Maybe I was imagining the flash and hadn't seen anything at all?

For the next minute, the cabin stayed annoyingly dark. I glanced around the parking area and scanned the nearby woods. Still no Matt. He'd said he'd be here, so where was he?

Then I remembered: Out on the ice, there was

no cell service. What if he wasn't responding because he was at the ice cabin? What if he hadn't received my text?

I'd promised him I wouldn't dawdle when I got here — that I'd take the decoy metal box to the ice cabin and leave immediately. He'd been particularly insistent on this point. He wanted me far, far away from the lake when the killer showed up.

At one point during our protracted negotiations, he'd pushed hard for Deputy Martinez to handle Task Three instead of me.

"That won't work," I'd replied calmly, hoping I was coming across as rational and measured.

"Why not?"

"Because we don't know what other technology is available to this secret spy organization." I pointed to the sky. "Like drones. Or even satellites."

He snorted. "Really? Drones? Flying over Eagle Cove?"

"My point is, we don't know. We should assume the worst."

He sighed. "We can dress her to look like you."

"That will take time we don't have and also prevent her from doing all of the other things your team needs to do to get ready."

"Sarah, I —"

"We can do this," I said. "It'll work out. I'll text you the instant I get there and the instant I leave. I'll be in and out in a flash."

And it was only then, with a long, heavy sigh, that he relented.

And it was only now, as I looked anxiously around the deserted parking lot, that I wondered whether I'd negotiated too well.

Did I want to be here? *No.*

Did I want to uphold my commitment to Matt and get this over with as quickly as possible? *Yes.*

Would I much rather be at Mom's house at this very moment, sitting down at the kitchen table for a hearty helping of her delicious lasagna? *Most definitely yes.*

Then it was time to get moving.

Energized, I removed the old toolbox from my handbag and, after a moment's consideration, wrapped the red scarf around it. On the off-chance that a drone actually was watching me from above — a ridiculous thought, of course, but better safe than sorry — I wanted it to see me carrying an object that looked like it could be the metal box.

I pushed open the car door and set out for the ice cabin, bundle in hand.

For the third time in twenty-four hours, I was doing something I'd never imagined myself doing. How strange and unpredictable life could be. The walk across the ice, though clumsy and slow, seemed almost familiar now, like a normal part of my routine. The wind tonight wasn't as intense, but the sky was darker and the air colder. Though the box in my arms wasn't heavy, it seemed weighted with significance.

We'd gone to a lot of trouble to catch this killer. Though my role in this effort was about to end, Matt and his deputies had a long, cold night ahead of them. As I neared the ice cabin, I found myself hoping our hard work would pay off.

In the cabin's window, I caught a hint of light behind the curtain. My pace picked up.

When I reached the cabin door, I pulled it open and saw Matt standing in the kitchen.

But wait — no.

When the man turned toward me, I realized he wasn't Matt.

The man was someone else.

And he was holding a speargun.

Aimed at me.

I froze with disbelief.

And lying on the ice at his feet, silent and still —

I saw Matt!

CHAPTER 19

"Step inside, Ms. Boone," the man said. His voice echoed in my head — a bad dream come to terrifying life.

I stood frozen, my eyes unable to move from the sight of Matt on the ground, silent and still, blood flowing from his head.

The man gestured with the gun. "Get in here."

"I need to check on him," I said, my heart pounding.

"No you don't. I clocked him good, but he's still alive."

"But —"

"Now!"

Trembling, I stepped inside and shut the door behind me. As I approached Matt's unconscious form, I blinked back a rush of tears when I saw his chest moving. He was breathing. The killer was right — *Matt was alive.*

"Move into the center of the room," the man said.

I did as ordered. As I stepped past him, I saw he was standing next to a gaping ice hole in the kitchen floor — a hole big enough to climb in and out of.

The man was wearing a wetsuit, I realized. His dark hair was wet. Next to the hole were a scuba tank and a mask.

And stacked on the dining table, still wet and glistening, were three more metal boxes, identical to the one Tony had given me.

Regret stabbed through me. The metal box in my basement wasn't the only one.

There were *more.*

It was a possibility I hadn't even considered.

But the killer had. He'd known. Not only that, he'd acted faster and gotten here first.

And now we were trapped.

With horror, I saw I was repeating history. Once again, due to my own unique blend of hubris and ignorance, I was alone with a killer while someone I loved lay unconscious at my feet. Except this time, unlike three months earlier in the basement of my aunt's building, there would be no inquisitive cat creating a distraction, no neighbors hearing me upstairs and calling the sheriff, and — my heart lurched — no sheriff preparing to storm the basement to rescue me.

Because my rescuer was lying eight feet from me, unconscious on the ice, blood flowing from his head....

"I hate this town," the killer said.

I blinked, his words startling me out of my regrets. "Excuse me?"

"This town is the worst."

My heart thumped. The killer wanted to talk, and that was good — *because talk meant hope*. "What's wrong with Eagle Cove?"

"Insufferable meddlers. All of you. Poking your noses into things that are none of your business."

I looked at his face — really looked at his face — and realized he was one of the security guards from the Applied Sciences building. He was in his late thirties, tall and beefy with dark hair, a former athlete going to seed. His forehead was creased with worry. In his dark eyes I saw anger and tension.

I had to draw him out. "You were expecting us. How did you know?"

"How do you think?"

I decided to act like his question was genuine. With as much calmness as I could muster, I said, "The sheriff and I hatched this little plan barely two hours ago, while sitting in my car." When he didn't respond, I continued. "You might have tapped into his communications with his deputies, but my bet is you bugged my car." I waited again but got no response. "You probably did that when I barged into your building and had my little scene. While the other guard was dealing with me, you stuck a GPS tracker on my car. That much I'd already figured. But you also wired the interior for sound. How am I doing?"

He sighed. "All of you think you're so smart."

"The food delivery last night was a surprise, wasn't it?" I continued, hazarding a guess. "The delivery interrupted you."

"That old biddy at the Golden Dragon," he said, disgusted. "All those questions."

I realized he was talking about Mrs. Chan. "You mean, when she asked your colleagues about themselves...."

"And Howard couldn't shut his trap. Never could. Told her about the ice fishing, and she told him they delivered everywhere, even on the ice. None of this would have happened if he'd kept his lips zipped."

"You didn't know he ordered delivery, did you?"

"I should have," he said. "He loved that food."

"You thought you had all night here at the ice cabin to recover the rest of your haul" — I gestured to the three metal boxes — "and stage the crime scene and get away before anyone had a clue."

"Operational oversight."

"The Golden Dragon wasn't the only one.

Howard also ordered breakfast muffins from my cafe. I delivered them myself, probably not long after you left."

"Lucky for you the kid got here first."

My stomach clenched as his meaning sank in. "Because I wouldn't have been able to escape?"

"The kid can move." *Unlike you*, he didn't say.

I flashed to the fear in Tony's eyes. "He can't identify you, by the way. He never saw your face."

He sneered. "No need to be vague, Ms. Boone. The kid's got a name. Tony Chan, sixteen years old, a junior at Eagle Cove High. I know who he is."

"What I'm saying is, you don't have to go after him."

"I should take your word?"

"You're the expert, so you decide — am I telling you the truth?"

He stared at me for a few seconds. "You might be." The sneering tone had dropped away, which I took as an encouraging sign.

"I think I know what happened here," I said, "but I probably have some of it wrong."

When he didn't reply, I pressed on, hoping he'd let me continue.

"I don't know what's in the metal boxes and I don't know how they ended up in the lake, but your colleagues knew. They decided to go after the boxes on their own, without the knowledge of your organization. I'm guessing they brought you in because they needed help getting something in or out of the building you all work in, or because you know how to scuba dive and they didn't. How am I doing so far?"

When he didn't tell me to shut up, I pointed to the diving gear. "You and your colleagues realized the ice cabin would be an excellent base of operations for your underwater retrieval. Once you had your treasure, the plan was to sell it and split the proceeds, and your organization would never know."

Again, I got no reply, but I could tell from the way his eyes flickered that I had his interest.

"Your three colleagues didn't know you had a plan of your own. You'd decided to betray them and keep the proceeds for yourself."

"They would have been caught," he said. "I had no choice."

Finally a response, and a defensive one at that. Was I detecting a hint of a guilty conscience? "So you killed them. I don't know how you did it, at least not exactly. There wasn't much blood in here, so I'm betting you didn't shoot or stab them or bash their heads in."

Involuntarily I glanced at Matt, still unmoving on the ground barely eight feet away, and pushed back my fears before they could overwhelm me.

Trying to keep my voice steady, I said, "I'm

guessing you slipped something into their drinks and drugged them."

His mouth twitched — I'd gotten that right.

"Then you pushed them through the ice hole and drowned them."

"They didn't suffer."

"Howard did."

"That was his fault."

"His fault?" I repeated, adding skepticism to my tone. "Because he woke up too soon?"

He blinked at that. Yes, he regretted the murders, at least to a certain extent. But was he regretting them enough to not kill me and Matt?

I pushed on. "I see a couple of explanations for how Howard got that spear in him. One is that he helped you drug the other two and then you speared him. Another is that you drugged him and he woke up before you could push him under the ice and you were forced to improvise."

He stared at me but didn't reply.

"There's one thing I don't get," I said.

"What's that?" He glanced at his watch, then returned his gaze to me.

"Why you deliberately hooked the three men to the fishing lines. The way you did it — hooks in the ear, eyebrow, and lip — is obviously a message. A clear reference to 'Hear no evil, see no evil, speak no evil.'"

I waited for a reply before adding, "I'm sure there's a story there."

"The story would take more time than we have."

"Your organization wronged you."

He grunted. "In more ways than you can imagine."

"The anger you carry —"

"Look," he said, "I get what you're doing. I'd do the same. I'd try to draw me out, get me talking, establish a bond, make me see you as a real person."

"This doesn't have to escalate further."

"You seem okay, actually." He sighed, but his aim didn't waver. "Reasonable. Normal. I can't say that about most of the people I work with."

"And you're saying this because…?"

"Just my way of saying this isn't personal."

"You have *got* to be kidding," I shot back, my voice rising. "This is *very* personal. Someone I care about is unconscious and bleeding on the ice. You're pointing a weapon at me and threatening to kill me."

"My point," he said, "is that none of this is about you. You're collateral."

I stared at him in disbelief. "And that's okay? Innocent people as collateral is *okay*?"

He looked like he wanted to argue but managed

to check himself. "I need you to tell me what you told Claire."

"Your colleague Claire, you mean, who I bet you've worked with for years? My childhood friend Claire, who I grew up with? Is she one of the so-called 'evil' ones you're so upset about?"

"No," he said. "But I can't let her get in my way."

"Why would I tell you anything? Why would I help you turn her into 'collateral'?"

"Your cooperation could save her life."

"You mean, save her from you."

"I'll throw in the kid, too."

"Meaning what?"

"I won't go after the kid. Or the old lady."

I went still. He was referring to Mrs. Chan and Tony. And I recalled what I'd forgotten to ask Tony earlier, when he mentioned Howard and his colleagues having dinner at the Golden Dragon. I'd meant to ask Tony how many people were with Howard. Now I knew the answer was three — the other two dead men and the killer.

"I'm supposed to believe a man who's already killed three times."

"Do you have a choice?"

I swallowed, scrambling for something to grab hold of. "I do have a choice. I have to decide whether I should accept the word of a man who's capable of truly despicable, gross acts. And I'm not just talking about the murders."

It took him a second, but he got it. "The hooks."

"Hooking your victims to the fishing lines was disgusting. Also gratuitous and disrespectful and excessive and just plain *creepy*."

"It was deliberate," he said, his voice rising.

Finally, I'd gotten under his skin. "Deliberately pointless. You did it for *kicks*."

His nostrils flared. "You have no idea what H.U.S.H. is like."

I'd just learned the name of the secret organization he worked for, I realized. "Try me. Tell me how 'evil' your employer really is."

"I —" he said, then stopped himself.

"Still covering for them," I said, with as much scorn as I could muster. "Can't help yourself, can you? Pathetic."

His eyes flashed with anger.

"Even now, you can't get them out of your head. Even now, you're letting them run the show."

"This was supposed to be my escape," he said, struggling to regain control. "Everything was laid out perfectly. And then that kid showed up with the delivery...."

"So instead of staying to fight the evil you claim to hate so much, you decided to vanish with those," I said, gesturing to the three boxes on the dining table. "I'm guessing your new identity is already lined up. Along with a buyer for the boxes."

"The rot goes too deep. You can't fight it. Escape is the only option."

"You could have reached out to Claire."

"Nah." He waved the speargun dismissively. "She would have choked."

"You mean, she wouldn't have gone along with your plan to murder innocent people?"

He grunted with impatience. "Time's up. What did you tell her?"

I pretended to weigh the choice I was making. "You won't go after Tony or Mrs. Chan?"

"I won't."

"And Claire?"

"Not as long as she stays out of my way."

I gave him a nod. "I told Claire about the metal box, but she hasn't seen it."

"Did you open it?"

I shook my head.

"So you don't know what's inside?"

"Not a clue."

"And the kid?"

"Same."

He stared hard at me for a moment, as if making up his mind, then pointed to the box wrapped in the red scarf in my arms. "Hand it over."

"This?" I said, looking at the box cradled in my arms.

"Carefully."

That's when I saw I had one final card, one last chance before —

"Where do you want it?" I said, shifting the box and the scarf in my arms like I was uncertain what to do. I looked at him with what I hoped was a confused expression.

He pointed impatiently to the kitchen table, just a few short feet away. "Set it there."

"On the chair?" I said, stepping closer. "Or on the table?" I started trying to unwrap the box from the scarf. "Darn thing's getting tangled. You don't want the scarf, do you? Just the box, right?"

"Just put it on the table!"

"Okay," I said. "Just trying to get it all sorted — "

Without warning, I threw the box and scarf in his face.

Surprised, he reached out with both hands to catch it —

And the box hit the speargun, knocking the weapon out of his hands —

And with the scarf blocking his view —

I screamed and tried to tackle him —

And when he shifted to avoid the charge, he slipped on the wet ice —

And we both tumbled down.

Frantically, I crawled away from him. My hand closed on the speargun. I whirled around, still flat on the ice, and looked up as he rose to his feet.

Enraged, he stepped toward me as I aimed the speargun at him —

And fired.

I hit him!

He cried out in pain and staggered backward as the spear went through his shoulder.

For a long moment, the only thing I heard was both of us panting heavily. He stared at me and I at him, both of us stunned.

"Ow," he said angrily, his cold dark eyes fixed on me.

Terror rocketed through me. I'd hurt him but hadn't stopped him — in fact, I'd barely slowed him.

And my speargun was out of spears.

He grasped the spear and was about to yank it out of his shoulder when I heard a voice behind him — a voice I'd feared I would never hear again — growl:

"Touch that spear and I'll drop you."

The man went still.

I gasped as Matt struggled to sit up. He leaned against the kitchen cabinet, blood running from his scalp, his face pale. His gun was out and aimed at the man.

"Matt!" I cried. He looked terrible — *but alive.*

His hand was steady and so was his voice. "On your knees. Turn to the wall. Hands behind your head."

The man didn't move.

"*Now.*"

The man obeyed and I scrambled past him to Matt's side. "I've never been so happy to hear your voice."

"Same," he said. "Do me a favor and call it in."

I whipped out my phone and stared at it. "No service here."

"Go to shore. Call from there."

"You sure?"

"Go. Now."

"You're still bleeding."

"A scalp wound."

"And your skull?"

"Still in one piece."

"Are you sure?"

"Sarah," he said, his voice urgent yet steady all at once. "Go call it in *now.*"

CHAPTER 20

The next few moments worked out as hoped, thank goodness. After rushing to shore, getting a signal, and calling 911, I raced back to the cabin and found Matt and the killer in the exact same spots I'd left them.

The deputies arrived a few moments later, followed by medics who loaded Matt and the killer onto stretchers and then rolled them across the ice to waiting ambulances. When I tried to climb into the ambulance with Matt, the medics shooed me out and Deputy Wilkerson told me apologetically that I needed to stay to help with the investigation.

"Sarah, I'll be fine," Matt said as the medics strapped his stretcher in. "I promise."

"Call as soon as you can," I said, trying to keep the anxiety out of my voice. "I need to know you're okay."

"Will do," he said with a reassuring smile. Heart in my throat, I watched his ambulance race away into the night.

Very gently, Deputy Wilkerson escorted me to his truck and talked me through the evening's events while he scribbled notes for my statement. After that came the usual slog — more waiting, more repeating, followed by more waiting and more repeating — as one officer after another asked me question after question after question.

Eventually, thank goodness, interest in me faded and I found myself momentarily alone. I was scanning the small crowd of onlookers outside the police barricade when I spied a familiar face — that of the security guard I'd chatted with at the Applied Sciences building.

When he saw that I'd seen him, he gestured toward a quiet spot at the far end of the parking area. After a quick look around, I joined him.

"Are you all right?" he asked when I got there, his eyes and tone conveying a concern that I sensed was real. Beneath his winter coat, he was shivering. Maybe what he'd told me about being from Atlanta was actually true. I wondered how long he'd been waiting to speak with me.

"I'm fine," I said quietly.

"How's your friend the sheriff?"

"He got hit on the head pretty bad. There was a

lot of blood." I willed myself to keep calm. "But I'm pretty sure he's going to be okay."

"Scalp wounds bleed a lot and can look a lot scarier than they really are," he said, trying to reassure me. "I understand he regained consciousness and is thinking clearly?"

"Yes."

"That's good."

"As soon as they let me out of here, I'm heading to the hospital."

The guard glanced around to make sure no was listening, then asked, "How badly hurt was … the other guy?"

He'd almost said the man's name, I realized.

"Your colleague, you mean," I said, unable to avoid the sudden rush of anger.

"Former colleague. What he did was inexcusable."

The contempt in his tone was impossible to miss. With a start, I realized the damage the killer had caused likely extended far beyond the actions I was aware of.

I cleared my throat. "I shot him with a spear. In the shoulder. The spear went all the way through. He's hurt, but he'll be fine."

I caught a glint of something — appreciation? satisfaction? — in the guard's eyes. He glanced around to make sure we weren't being overheard, then said, "You told me your name earlier today but I didn't tell you mine. I'm Edgar."

I blinked with surprise. "You're Edgar? Claire's colleague Edgar?"

"Thank you for not asking for me earlier."

"I almost did."

"Why didn't you?"

It took me a few seconds to sort through my thoughts. "I basically understand nothing about your world. So if I have to be involved, I have to trust someone. And that someone is Claire."

His gaze was steady as he waited for me to continue.

"If Claire says I can trust you, then trust you I will."

"And you didn't ask for me today because…?"

"Because I didn't know you were Edgar. And because the instant I set foot in the lobby, I sensed I was in danger. I realized just in time that if I mentioned you, I'd be putting you in danger as well."

"You understand that going there today was —"

"A mistake," I said, shuddering at how close I'd come to disaster.

Edgar shrugged. "I was about to say 'a catalyst.' You shook the tree and got results. Risk isn't only about danger. It's also about reward."

"From now on, I'm leaving the risk and reward to you and Claire."

He gave me a smile. "She and I spoke a few moments ago. She arrives tomorrow morning."

"I can't wait to see her."

"I assume the final box is...?"

"Safe," I assured him. "I'll give it to her tomorrow." I gestured across the parking lot to the three metal boxes stacked on the cold ground, waiting to be tagged and bagged by the crime-scene technicians. "Do you need any help with...?"

"We're good. They'll be back in our possession shortly."

I waited for him to elaborate on how he planned to accomplish that task, but of course he didn't. "Back?"

He smiled. "Slip of the tongue."

I doubted that. "Any idea what's in them?"

"No idea."

"Doesn't that worry you?"

His eyebrows rose. "Should it?"

"What if the boxes contain something bad?"

"They easily could."

"Aren't you worried how they might be used? I don't know much about H.U.S.H., but what I do know isn't exactly reassuring."

He tensed. "How do you know that name?"

"The killer said it."

He frowned, clearly not pleased. "Best you forget you heard it."

"You're not going to tell me anything, are you?"

"Most definitely not, Ms. Boone."

"You know, since we're basically almost friends now, you should call me Sarah."

"Sarah," he said, his tone still serious. "This is one of those times when a little bit of knowledge can be a very dangerous thing. Promise me you won't tell anyone —"

"That I know that name? Got it. Never heard it. My lips are zipped. I swear I'll keep totally hush-hush about you-know-what."

He stared at me, perturbed by my flippancy, then sighed. "About your statement to the deputy."

"No worries. I somehow forgot to mention anything related to your secret employer."

"Thank you. But will your friend the sheriff…?"

"You're good there."

"How can you be sure?"

"He and Claire go way back, too."

He regarded me for a long moment. "Thank you."

"It'll be gold, I think."

He blinked, thrown by the change in topic. "Gold?"

"Sunken treasure. That's what I'll tell everyone the four men were after."

Comprehension dawned. "Ah."

"I'll keep it vague. Throw in speculation about old Spanish doubloons or some such. People love to talk and theorize and connect dots. I'll come up with a mystery they can really dig their teeth into."

At that moment, a familiar voice called my name and I turned to see Mom at the barricade, scanning the scene for me.

"I should go," I said as I turned back to Edgar —

And found he'd already vanished.

"Sarah!" Mom yelled anxiously, waving me over.

After a quick look around — Edgar had somehow managed to disappear into the night — I ran up to Mom and gave her a hug.

"You look so cold," Mom said, her grip like a vise. "Are you in shock? Has Doc Barnes examined you?"

"I'm fine, Mom."

She let me go and whirled on Deputy Wilkerson, who at that moment was manning the barricade. "Young man, I'm taking my daughter home."

"Ma'am —"

"Don't you 'ma'am' me, young man. My daughter is cold and tired. She needs to get out of this freezing weather. She'll be staying with me tonight. You have her number and mine. You can call if you have questions."

After a helpless shrug — because what else

could he do in the face of such maternal determination? — the deputy acquiesced.

"We'll be going to the hospital first," I told him as I headed out. "To check on Matt. I'll call you with an update as soon as I know more."

CHAPTER 21

The next morning at the cafe, after the usual early crowd of caffeine cravers and muffin munchers flowed in and away, the gang packed themselves into Gabby's booth for the inside scoop on all that had gone down. Gabby, Mr. Benson, and Hialeah were there, of course, joined this morning by Mrs. Chan and Tony.

It had been a long and exhausting night. After leaving the crime scene, Mom and I had rushed to the hospital and were allowed to see Matt briefly. As the nurses fussed over him, we learned they were keeping him overnight for observation (due to a likely concussion) but were expecting him to make a full recovery.

After Mom pulled me away, gently but firmly, she took me home. While she heated up a batch of her delicious lasagna, I called Anna and Grace and told them all about my very busy twenty-four hours (minus the spy stuff, of course). Then I called Janie and updated her as well.

More calls came after that — the mayor calling for Mom, Wendy Danvers calling for me — but as the adrenaline rush faded and exhaustion crept in, I found it harder to focus on anything other than the lasagna that would soon emerge from the oven.

When it finally did, its rich, heavenly aroma filling the kitchen, my stomach roared into full rumble mode. Plates in hand, Mom led me into the living room, turned on the TV, and settled us on the couch. I'd barely finished my plate — mmm, so good — when I dozed off, comfy and warm under a blanket, Mom at my side. At some point, she roused me and guided me upstairs to my childhood bedroom, where I managed to set my alarm before immediately crashing.

So the following morning, as I stood at the cash register in the cafe, I could only marvel at all that had happened. Two days earlier, Howard Penn had walked into Emily's Eats and ordered muffins for delivery. Two days later, he and his colleagues were dead, I'd almost been murdered, and the killer was in custody.

My thoughts were interrupted by a familiar and impatient voice. "Sarah," Gabby yelled. "Stop dawdling and get over here!"

"Now, Gabby," Mr. Benson said, coming to my

defense. “She’ll get here in due time. She has a cafe to run, after all.”

“What would you know about *running*, old man?”

“Woman, I —“

“There in a sec,” I called out. Just then, Janie emerged from the kitchen with the morning edition of the *Gazette.*

“Meant to show you this earlier,” she murmured.

The lead story, hot off the presses and written by Wendy Danvers, was headlined “Suspect apprehended in Lake killings.” The article proved a concise write-up of what the sheriff and local prosecutor knew about the case.

“Seems fine,” I said cautiously. “Nothing to worry about.”

“Go to the editorial,” Janie said.

I sighed. The *Gazette* was run by Bob Underhill, and Bob was a conspiracy nut who used his editorials to warn us about various secret machinations by shadowy corporate and government forces. I was quite familiar with his screeds — they were often entertaining, in an over-the-top way — but what he’d published today had Janie worried. Pulse quickening, I opened to the second page and read:

A functioning democracy requires not only the active participation of its citizens, but a commitment from those in power to govern transparently.

Sadly, all too often, our leaders fail to live up to their part of the deal. Instead of leveling with us, they hide, lie, and obfuscate. They bury their secrets behind walls of denial.

In doing so, our leaders ignore a fundamental truth: Secrets do not wish to remain buried. Secrets yearn for the light. Hidden in the darkness, they fester and mutate and grow in power. And when, inevitably, they burst forth, their fury often knows no bounds.

The shocking murders of three men on Heartsprings Lake are a sad and unnecessary case in point. The men, who were linked to our government in ways we do not yet fully comprehend, were searching for something beneath the lake's icy waters. Something secret, dangerous, and deadly. What that something is, we do not yet know.

But mark my words, citizens of Eagle Cove: The Gazette *will not cease in its efforts to find out.*

Nothing less than the fate of our democracy rests on our ability to shine the cleansing light of truth on the secrets that the powerful seek to hide.

I tried to squelch a rush of anxiety. After all that had just happened, Bob's words (though a tad thunderous and melodramatic for my taste) hit uncomfortably close to home.

But I couldn't let that show. With what I hoped

was an air of patient amusement, I said, "Oh, that's just Bob being Bob."

Janie's anxious eyes held mine, unconvinced. "Okay," she finally replied.

I gestured to the booth. "Come on, let's update the gang while it's quiet."

Janie and I pulled up chairs. As quickly and thoroughly as I could, I gave them a full recap of the night's action, leaving out only the spy angle and the metal boxes.

"Oh, dear," Mr. Benson said when I got to the speargun tussle. "I don't like the sound of that."

"Well, I do," Gabby declared. "The maniac deserved it."

"What in the world was he after?" Mrs. Chan asked.

Tony and I exchanged a quick look. "Well," I said, lowering my voice and acting like I wasn't supposed to be sharing what I was about to share. "It appears the killer was in league with the three victims. The four of them were working together to recover something from the lake."

"What were they after?" Mr. Benson asked.

"Gold, apparently. Buried treasure — I guess you could say sunken treasure — of some sort."

Mrs. Chan gasped and Mr Benson murmured, "You don't say."

I glanced briefly at Tony and sensed his silent approval.

I continued. "The investigators are looking at a bank robbery that took place in Boston twenty years ago. The crooks broke into safe deposit boxes and got away with ten million dollars in rare coins, including antique gold Spanish doubloons. The loot was never found."

I waited to see if the idea took hold. The robbery I'd mentioned had in fact occurred — I'd found a nice little write-up on a true-crime site before coming into the cafe — but I knew that convincing this crowd could take some doing.

Gabby was frowning. "Gold doubloons? In Heartsprings Lake?"

"It's just a theory," I said, trying to sound cautious. "But apparently one of the victims had old newspaper clippings about the robbery in his possession."

Gabby's eyebrows rose. "Well, if that's the case...."

"It would explain so much," Mrs. Chan said eagerly. "The four of them certainly acted like they were hiding something when they came to the Golden Dragon for dinner."

"Why did they think the gold's in the lake?" Mr. Benson asked.

"No idea," I replied. "The three dead men were scientists, so they knew how to research stuff. And one was apparently a true-crime buff, so maybe that's how it started? One thing we know for sure is how they knew each other. They all worked in the same building at Middlemore. The killer was a security guard there and knew how to scuba dive, which may be why the three scientists brought him in."

"And after they brought him in, he betrayed them," Mr. Benson said.

"Yes," I said heavily. "Of that part, at least, there's no doubt."

"Why did the killer go back to the lake?" Gabby asked, still not convinced. "And why were you and the sheriff there?"

I'd anticipated the questions. "Matt asked me to return to the crime scene because something about the case — I'm not sure what, to be honest — was nagging at him." I paused to see how that played, then went on. "I'm pretty sure he was hoping that, if I stepped back inside, something would be jogged loose from my memory."

"Did it work?" Gabby asked.

I shook my head. "The killer was there when I got there. He'd just gotten out of the water. He'd been scuba-diving again, looking for the treasure."

Mrs. Chan squeezed her grandson's arm. "I'm so grateful you and Tony survived."

"Same here," Tony chimed in.

"Me, too," I said, very truthfully. "I can't tell you how glad I am to be here right now, safe and sound, surrounded by my friends."

"Hear, hear," Mr. Benson said.

"Darn tootin'," Gabby threw in.

"Sarah," Hialeah said, "how's Matt doing?"

"He's fine." I took a quick breath to steady my voice. "I called first thing this morning and we spoke. He has a nasty cut on his scalp — twenty stitches — along with a concussion and a hairline skull fracture, so the hospital's keeping him another night for observation. But he's expected to fully recover. He sounded good. I'll be visiting tonight after closing up."

"I am so relieved, Sarah," Hialeah said.

I was about to agree when the cafe door burst open and Claire swept in, luggage in tow, looking her usual terrific self — tall and slim, blonde and elegant. My spirits soared at the sight of her.

"Good morning, everyone!" she exclaimed cheerfully. Surprised and delighted, the gang roared their welcome. Janie jumped to her feet and pulled her in for a hug. "Claire, I had no idea!"

It was only in the quick glance Claire gave me while hugging Janie that I caught a hint of the tension and tiredness she was carrying. She'd traveled nearly a day to get here, at the behest of a secret organization riddled with treachery and dissension. I could only imagine how much stress she was feeling beneath her energetic facade.

"I'm so glad to be here," she said brightly. "It's so good to see you all. Sorry I didn't tell you I was coming — I only just found out. There was an unexpected hiccup in the data-center project at Middlemore." She gave me a smile. "Is what I'm hearing true? That I missed out on some excitement?"

"Did you ever," Gabby said. "Take a load off and we'll fill you in."

Mr. Benson scooted over to make room. "If rumors are true, there might be sunken treasure in Heartsprings Lake. Gold, in fact. Ten million dollars' worth."

"Gold?" Claire repeated, eyes widening. Her gaze flickered toward me.

I gave her a grin. "That's what the authorities are saying, or so I hear. I'll get you a nice big mocha latte while they tell you all about it."

CHAPTER 22

The smile didn't leave my face as I made Claire's mocha. The gang's rendition of my manufactured tale was vivid and skillful — even exciting. With luck, the Eagle Cove gossip network would grab hold of the buried treasure theory and run with it.

An influx of late-morning customers pulled me and Janie away from the gang, but the conversation in the booth continued full steam. I'd just finished handing a customer his blueberry scone when I realized Hialeah was standing beside me, waiting for a moment to speak.

"Hialeah," I said, glancing toward the still-lively conversation in the booth. "I'm glad you're here. I was hoping for a private word."

Hialeah waited for me to continue, her gaze patient and knowing.

"It's about what you said yesterday." I took a deep breath. "You were pretty much basically totally completely right."

She shrugged. "I wish I could have been more specific."

"I need to apologize."

"Apologize?"

"For doubting you."

"Sarah," she said gently. "There's no need for that."

"No, there is. I've always assumed that what psychics do is … well, a combination of psychology and observation and not much else. From now on, at least when it comes to you, consider me a reformed skeptic."

"Thank you," she said quietly. "I only hope I can do better next time."

My eyes widened. "Next time?"

She nodded sadly. "I'm afraid my work in Eagle Cove is not yet done."

I gulped — her words sounded so ominous — and I was about to dig further when Claire got up from the booth and announced she had to get over to Middlemore.

"Sarah," she said, looking over at me. "Would it be all right if…?"

I grinned. "If you stayed in the studio apartment upstairs?"

Claire gave me a smile.

"Of course. It's ready and waiting."

"Thank you — I really appreciate it." She turned to the gang. "I'm so glad to be back in Eagle Cove. Mrs. Chan and Tony, great meeting you."

I popped my head into the kitchen, told Janie I was taking Claire upstairs, then led Claire into the building hallway. After shutting the cafe door and waiting a moment to ensure we weren't going to be followed, I said quietly, "It's in the basement."

Claire's eyebrows rose. "Not where I expected, given how much you hate being down there."

"Well, I hate the metal box, too. So I suppose there's a certain symmetry."

A minute later, with a huge sense of relief, I handed her the box, grateful it was no longer my responsibility.

I looked around, suppressing a shudder. Claire was right about me disliking this space. The musty air, dusty shelves, and poor lighting would forever evoke memories of danger and death.

Claire held the box closer to the light of the single overhead bulb to examine it more closely.

"Why did Howard want you to have it?" I asked.

She shrugged. "Probably last-minute regrets."

"You mean, he knew he was going to die, and suddenly was sorry for what he'd set in motion?"

"It happens. People find clarity, even resolve, in their final moments."

"Do you know what's in the boxes?"

"I've been told what's in them," she said carefully.

"But you have doubts. You're not sure if what you've been told is true."

She sighed. "What I know is that the boxes have a history, going back decades."

"And you know this because…?"

"Because ever since the first one was discovered, upper management has been reaching out to retired agents and reactivating them."

"Like they did with Aunt Emily."

Her expression was serious. "Decades ago, something important and probably very bad happened. Whatever that something was got buried."

"But now it's back."

"With a vengeance."

"And folks are freaking."

"Pretty much," she sighed.

"How are you holding up? I'm sensing a certain tension."

She shrugged, the tiredness in her eyes unmistakable. "I'm fine. But yes, there's a lot going on."

"Which you can't tell me about."

"It's best you not know."

"I get that. And this time, I really mean it."

She stared at me for a long moment, assessing the truthfulness of that statement.

"Well," she finally said. "I hope so." She bent down, unzipped her luggage, and stuffed the metal box inside.

"How long are you here?"

"Just today and tonight." She zipped her suitcase tight and stood up. "You know," she said, her tone lighter, "you're gaining a reputation in certain circles."

"Oh, am I?"

"Code names are being floated." She gave me a smile. "'Traitor Trapper' is a contender."

I grinned and shook my head. "Nah. Not catchy enough."

"Edgar was impressed, by the way."

"With?"

"You. The way you handled yourself."

"Glad to hear," I replied, pleased. "He seems like a nice fellow. I felt bad for him last night."

"Why's that?"

"Poor thing was shivering out there in the cold night air. He needs to dress more warmly."

Claire smiled. "I'll see that he does."

"He seemed rather protective toward you. Any chance you two are…?"

"Oh, no," she said right away, then paused before adding, "He's Ben's brother."

"Ah," I said slowly, the implications sinking in.

Her *ex-husband's* brother. I'd met Ben exactly twice — once at their wedding, and a second time at a casual dinner in L.A., about a year before their divorce. "So if Edgar is a secret agent and you're a secret agent, does that mean Ben is also….?"

She shrugged. "Makes for an interesting dynamic at work."

"You mean, you and Ben are still working together? I can't even begin to imagine."

"It's not bad or terrible or anything like that. We're both trying." She paused, struggling for words. "It's just … awkward at times."

She almost said more at that point. In that tiny sliver of a moment, we almost became best friends again. But she pulled back, perhaps concerned about drawing me even further into her dangerous world. "I have some good news," she said instead. She reached into her coat pocket and handed me a slip of paper. "This is for your mom."

Hope rushed through me. "Is this what I think it is?"

"It took a lot of wrangling," Claire said. "Your mom better not blow it."

"I'll do my best to impress that upon her."

"The only place this will work is inside her house."

"You did something there, didn't you?" I said, frowning. "Your tech wizard people broke in and installed secret spy stuff in my mother's house, didn't they?"

She gave me a shrug, her gaze steady and unconcerned.

"I can't believe you think it's necessary to spy on my *mom.*"

"This evening at six."

I looked again at the sheet of paper, then back up at her. "Thank you."

"No need to thank me." I caught a hint of a smile. "After all, as you made perfectly clear, I had no choice."

I grinned back. "No choice at all."

CHAPTER 23

That evening, after closing the cafe, I hopped into my car and drove to Mom's house. As I pulled up to the snug two-story house I was raised in, I reviewed the whopper I was about to tell — a story so ridiculous and absurd, it might just work — and found myself hoping for the best. Then I scooted inside and zipped into the kitchen, where I found Mom pulling leftover lasagna from the fridge.

"I assume you…?" she asked me, pointing to the lasagna.

"Absolutely." I glanced at the wall clock — it was time. "But first, I have a surprise."

"A surprise?"

I pointed to the kitchen table. "This is going to be a shock. A good shock, but still. I want you sitting down."

She looked at me curiously but complied. I grabbed her laptop, which was already on the kitchen table, and typed my way to the website that Claire had given me.

On the screen, a blank page appeared with login fields for a username and password.

Mom frowned as she watched me type in the credentials. "Don't tell me this is some new online dating service. I told you I'd do that only if and when I'm ready."

"Nope, not that. Though this does involve seeing someone incredible."

I entered the password and waited. A few seconds later, a video window popped up and we found ourselves looking at a beautifully decorated colonial-style study with large windows covered with plantation shutters.

There was a blur of movement. A figure sat down and faced the camera.

And Mom let out a huge gasp as Aunt Emily's angular face filled the screen.

"Emily!" she cried.

"Nancy," Emily said, her voice crisp and strong and full of emotion. "It's so wonderful to see you!"

Mom let out a huge whoop, her face alive with joy. "I knew it!" she exclaimed. "I knew it!"

I pulled Mom in for a hug, then grabbed a chair and settled in beside her to gaze at the woman I'd last seen three months earlier in a hospital bed, bandaged and in pain. Through the video screen, Emily looked healthy and vigorous, her skin tanned, her eyes alive with feeling. In every respect, the aunt I knew and loved was *back*.

"You're looking great," I said.

"Thank you, Sarah. I'm receiving wonderful care here."

"Where is *there*, Emily?"

"I'm at a private clinic in Costa Rica."

I wondered how close to the truth that was. "Costa Rica? What are you doing down there?"

"A long story. But first, Nancy, you said you knew. What did you know?"

Mom was still doing a happy dance in her chair. "I knew you were alive! I knew it!"

"Wait," I said, trying to help. "You mean you were *hoping* she was alive?"

"Well, of course I was hoping that. But no, I *knew*."

Emily and I exchanged a glance. To prepare for this moment, I'd come up with what I considered to be a ludicrous lie to explain how Emily hadn't died in a fiery car crash. In the lie, Emily had spent the past four months in a coma, receiving specialized medical care at a private clinic run by a very rich old Swiss friend of hers whom she'd met back in her days of international travel. The crispy corpse found in Emily's car was actually another friend of theirs who'd been visiting Emily at the time. Emily's rich old Swiss friend had very particular ideas about law enforcement and was used to getting his way and hadn't bothered to tell anyone when he whisked Emily by private jet to his clinic. And now that she was finally conscious and recovering, Emily couldn't wait to reconnect with her loved ones. But there was a catch: She didn't want to get her Swiss friend in trouble. If the authorities found out what he'd done, he'd be in a *lot* of trouble. So for the time being, no one could know she was alive. Her friend had saved her life — she owed him big-time. Which meant it was essential for Mom keep the news of Emily's survival to herself and for the rest of the world to continue to believe that Emily was dead and buried.

I'd run the lie by Claire earlier and received her seal of approval, and she'd promised to pass it along to Emily.

But now, depending on what Mom said next, it was possible that my ludicrous lie would need adjusting.

"I mean, at first I didn't know," Mom said with a laugh. "I thought they'd finally gotten you. I was a total mess for days — ask Sarah. But then I realized how convenient it all was."

"They?" I repeated, stunned.

"Our nation's enemies, of course."

Emily's eyes widened. "And when you say

'convenient,'" my aunt said carefully, "you're referring to…."

"The car crash. You know, your body being burned to a crisp. I mean, come on. How likely is that? I looked it up. The answer is — extremely unlikely! Cars don't burn up like that. That's only in the movies."

I realized my mouth was agape and shut it.

"And then, this one" — Mom continued, giving my arm a squeeze — "went on a long afternoon car ride with Claire and came back a different person. Suddenly she was happy and chipper."

"Mom," I said, feeling my entire world shift yet again. "What are you saying?"

"I'm saying I know about Emily and her past."

"Nancy," Emily said, clearly as shocked as I was. "I need you to tell me what you think you know."

Mom sighed. "You mean, about you and Ted traipsing around the globe? Supposedly for an oil company?" She let out a snort. "I never bought that."

Emily's eyes widened. "If that's the case, then why did you…."

"Why did I keep quiet?" Mom shrugged. "Mostly because I was so glad you'd moved back to Eagle Cove. I figured you'd tell me when you were ready. And when you never did, I realized you had no interest in bringing up the past — it was just too painful for you. So I stopped thinking about it. It became easier to go along with what you wanted everyone to believe."

I held my breath, watching Emily decide in real-time how best to handle this very unexpected curveball.

"Thank you, Nancy," Emily finally said. "I'm so sorry I held that back from you all these years."

"You have nothing to apologize for," Mom said. "*Nothing*. I can only imagine what a burden it must have been for you to keep that part of your life secret."

"You are so important to me, Nancy. I love you so much. I hope you know that."

"Oh, I do."

"I want you to know that Sarah is the one we have to thank for us talking right now."

Mom turned to me. "I was hoping you'd find a way."

I blinked with surprise. "Find a way?"

"That's your superpower, dear. You're relentless. You never let anything stop you, once you set your mind to something."

I pushed back a rush of tears. "Mom…."

"I assume Claire helped, too?"

"Claire?" I repeated, trying to sound confused.

"Oh, come on," Mom said. "Look at her. So stylish and confident. So mysterious and vague. Traveling all the time, just like Emily used to. Don't worry, her secret's safe with me."

"All of this needs to remain between us," Emily said. "You do understand that, Nancy?"

"Of course," Mom said immediately. "I'm excellent at keeping secrets." When Emily and I exchanged startled looks, Mom added indignantly, "Look at what I haven't been sharing with either of you for the past thirty years!"

"Mom, you're right," I said hastily. "I have every confidence in you. I know that Emily has a lot to tell you. And normally I'd stay here with the two of you, but…."

"But what, dear?" Emily said.

"I need to head to the hospital to see Matt."

Mom's eyes widened. "Of course." When I stood up, she rose with me and pulled me in for one of her trademark tight hugs.

"How is Matthew doing, Sarah?" Emily asked as I attempted to breathe.

"Fine, thankfully. He'll make a full recovery."

Mom released me and gave me a Mom-style visual inspection. "You're ready, aren't you?"

I gulped, surprised again. "Ready?"

"To take a chance again."

My voice sounded small. "You think so?"

"I do." Then she pulled me in for even more maternal squeezing.

"I'm actually basically terrified," I admitted, glancing over her shoulder at Emily. "But as someone very wise once told me, when it comes to matters of the heart, I can't be afraid to leap."

Emily smiled. "Matthew is a very lucky man."

With difficulty, I extricated myself from Mom's grip. "Talk to you soon, Aunt Emily?"

"Yes, very soon," Emily said, her eyes twinkling. "That's a promise."

CHAPTER 24

The hospital was quiet, the elevator empty aside from me. On the third floor, my winter boots squeaked slightly on the linoleum floor.

At the nurses' station, the duty nurse glanced up from her computer and smiled when she recognized me. "He's in Room 323."

"Thank you."

As I walked down the hallway, my heart started thumping. Was I ready for this? With a final burst of resolve, I stepped into Matt's room and found him in pajamas and bathrobe on his hospital bed, flipping through television channels, looking restless and bored.

His expressive grey eyes lit up when they landed on me. "Hey," he said, turning off the TV. "Thanks for coming by."

"You're looking good," I replied. Indeed, he

seemed rested and calm — pretty much normal aside from the bandage covering part of his head behind his left ear. "Certainly better than last night. Where is everyone? I was expecting a crowd."

"The crowd was here earlier. You just missed the boys. Betsy insisted on taking them home for dinner."

I smiled. "I don't know what your office would do without her."

"She's been really great today."

I stepped closer. "How are you feeling?"

"Fine. Well, mostly. My head hurts. But that's to be expected."

I gestured to the bandage. "How long will that be on?"

"They'll take out the stitches in a few days."

"Do they expect a scar?"

He shrugged. "It'll be under my hair, so no worries."

I felt nervous all of a sudden. No, not nervous — awkward. "Is the plan to keep you one more night?"

"I wanted to go home tonight, but they insisted, so...."

"I'm glad they're being cautious."

I'd come with a goal. But now that I was here, standing in front of him, the goal seemed impossible. I was taken aback when I heard myself say, "Can I ask you something?"

"Sure."

"What happened in the ice cabin after I left to call 911?"

"Not much," he said after a short pause. "It was kind of a waiting game. He was waiting for me to lose consciousness. I was waiting for him to make a move."

"If he'd made a move," I continued before I could stop myself, "would you have shot him?"

His expression became serious, his mouth settling in a firm line. "I've never fired my weapon in the line of duty. I hope I never have to. But to protect you, I wouldn't have hesitated."

Swallowing a rush of emotion, I reached out and took his hand in mine. He squeezed back, his touch strong and warm.

"I'm so glad you woke up when you did," I said. "I was out of spears."

He gazed at me steadily. "I'm pretty sure you would have come up with Plan B or Plan C or Plan Z. Whatever was needed, you'd have figured it out."

Touched by his faith, I felt tears of gratitude coming on. Without quite realizing what I was doing, I found myself climbing onto the bed next to him.

He scooted over, surprised, and remained completely still as I brought my lips to his and —

Kissed him softly.

Heart pounding, I pulled back and looked him in the eye.

"Sarah, what is this?" he whispered, his voice thick with emotion.

"It's me accepting what I want."

He blinked, his eyes brimming with emotion. "Please say you're not messing with me."

I shook my head slowly. "No messing. Not anymore."

"Anymore?"

I leaned in and kissed him again, still softly, but letting the kiss linger. He'd shaved earlier. Showered, too, judging by the hint of soap in his scent.

"I've been such an idiot," I whispered when I finally pulled away.

He reached up and caressed my cheek, just like he had all those years ago.

"Don't say that," he whispered, his body warm and solid next to mine.

"A scared idiot. After my divorce, I lost confidence in myself. I was afraid to try again because…."

"I get it. I've been there, too." He reached an arm around me and pulled me closer.

I swallowed a rush of emotion. "Part of me thought, maybe I don't deserve a second chance."

"What do you mean?"

"With you."

"Sarah…."

"Because of how I broke up with you."

"We were young. Both of us. Neither of us knew any better."

"Even now, twenty-five years later, there's so much I haven't figured out."

"Like what?"

"Like how not to make a mess of things. I mean, let's face it, I'm a messy mess who makes messes. The mayor called me a murder magnet."

He pulled back to look me square in my face, his eyes wide with surprise. "She called you *what*?"

Then he chuckled, and the chuckles turned to laughter.

My cheeks flamed hot. *What was going on?*

"You," he said, his grey eyes alive with amusement, "are many things. But a mess-making murder magnet you are not."

My eyes narrowed. "You better tell me why you're laughing."

His hand found my cheek again. "Here's what you are, Sarah Boone." In his clear grey eyes, I saw pleasure and affection and so much more. "You are, without question, the most exasperating, infuriating, challenging, amazing, incredible woman I've ever known."

A gasp escaped my lips.

"You're caring and thoughtful and generous and dedicated to your friends and family and community. You're ferocious about doing what's right, even if that means bending or ignoring or stomping all over the rules. You're smart and exciting and intuitive and impulsive and" — he leaned in and breathed in my ear, sending a tingle through me — "gorgeous as all get-out."

Oh, my. I felt myself flush.

"Since the day I met you, I've never stopped loving you."

Oh, my.

Then he pulled me in and kissed me again, his lips slow and lingering and incredible.

Eventually his mouth returned to my ear, his voice a husky whisper. "As soon as they let me out of this place, I'm taking you on a date. A real date."

I nearly purred at the thought. *Oh, my….*

"And then…."

When he whispered what he was going to do next, I could only think:

Oh my oh my oh my!

The End

MURDER SO PRETTY

EAGLE COVE MYSTERIES #3

Who knew flowers could be so *fatal?!?*

The annual Eagle Cove Flower Show is a huge deal in our little town, so when my cafe is hired to cater the opening reception, I'm determined to do everything I can to make the event a fun, festive, floral success.

All's going well until, amidst the revelry, I stumble upon the freshly murdered corpse of the head judge.

Now the town's in an uproar, media hordes are descending, and good friends are behaving very suspiciously.

With secrets swirling and loved ones in danger, I have no choice but to dig into this flowery, murdery mess —

Before the killer strikes again.

COMING SOON: MURDER SO TENDER

EAGLE COVE MYSTERIES #4

Who turned the barbeque into a *funeral pyre?!*

Eagle Cove's annual Fourth of July celebration is a cherished town tradition, filled with fireworks, fun, and favorite summer foods.

Then someone buries a body in the barbeque pit.

And with the lovely aroma of roasted pig comes an intriguing scent that folks can't quite put their finger on....

Murder So Tender is coming soon! To find out when, sign up for Nora's newsletter at AuthorNoraChase.com

BY THIS AUTHOR

AVAILABLE NOW OR COMING SOON

Heartsprings Valley Romances
by Anne Chase

Christmas to the Rescue!

A Very Cookie Christmas

Sweet Apple Christmas

I Dream of Christmas

Chock Full of Christmas

The Christmas Sleuth

Eagle Cove Mysteries
by Nora Chase

Murder So Deep

Murder So Cold

Murder So Pretty

Murder So Tender

Emily Livingston Mysteries
by Nora Chase

A Death in Barcelona

From Rome, With Murder

Paris Is for Killers

In London We Die

GET A FREE STORY!

A heartwarming holiday story about a handsome veterinarian and the shy, beautiful librarian he meets on Christmas Eve....

Nick and the Snowplow is a companion to *Christmas to the Rescue!*, the first novel in the Heartsprings Valley

Winter Tale series. In *Christmas to the Rescue!*, a young librarian named Becca gets caught in a blizzard on Christmas Eve, finds shelter with a handsome veterinarian named Nick, and ends up experiencing the most surprising, adventure-filled night of her life.

Nick and the Snowplow, told from Nick's point of view, shows what happens after Nick brings Becca home at the end of their whirlwind evening.

This story is available FOR FREE when you sign up for Anne Chase's email newsletter.

Go to AnneChase.com to sign up and get your free story.

ABOUT THE AUTHOR

As Anne Chase, I write small-town Christmas romances celebrating love during the most wonderful time of the year.

As Nora Chase, I write mysteries packed with murder, mayhem, and secrets galore.

My email newsletters are great ways to find out about my upcoming books.

Christmas romance: Sign up at AnneChase.com.

Mysteries: Sign up at AuthorNoraChase.com.

Thank you for being a reader.

Made in the USA
Monee, IL
23 July 2023